Do Over

Shannon Guymon

Bonneville Books
An Imprint of Cedar Fort, Inc.
Springville, Utah

This is a work of fiction. The characters, names, incidents, places, and dialogue are products of the author's imagination and are not to be construed as real.

ISBN 13: 978-1-4621-1154-1

Published by Bonneville Books an imprint of Cedar Fort, Inc., 2373 W. 700 S., Springville, UT 84663
Distributed by Cedar Fort, Inc., www.cedarfort.com

LIBRARY OF CONGRESS CATALOGING-IN-PUBLICATION DATA ON FILE

Cover design by Rebecca J. Greenwood
Cover design © 2013 by Lyle Mortimer
Edited by Whitney A. Lindsley and McKenzie Hansen
Typeset by Whitney A. Lindsley

Printed in the United States of America

10 9 8 7 6 5 4 3 2 1

To my children, Skyler, Savannah, Jessica, Kaleb, Tucker, and Ruby. I love you!

Other books by Shannon Guymon

Makeover

Taking Chances

The Broken Road

Forever Friends

Soul Searhing

Never Letting Go of Hope

A Trusting Heart

Justifiable Means

Prologue

I hate men," Iris whispered furiously as she gripped the woman's cell phone so hard one of the rhinestones popped off.

The woman gently pried her phone out of Iris's clenched, white hand. "Well, like I said, I just thought you should know. By the way, since I'm your new best friend, call me Cherish."

Iris glanced around her wedding reception and felt a cold, heavy dread settle over her shoulders. It went well with the misery, shock, and despair that were already suffocating her.

"Telling me yesterday would have been nice," she said softly as the lace on her wedding dress started to itch her arms.

The tall voluptuous blonde winced and stepped closer, looking like she was about to drop yet another bomb on the happiest day of Iris's life. "Look, I didn't even know about you until last night when Riley's *other* girlfriend confronted *me*. Some trashy girl named Germaine. An office assistant. So cliché. She knew all about you and was fine, but when she found out about me, that was too much I guess. And just for the record, I didn't know about either of you when I started seeing Riley. Trust me, I'm not the type to share. I don't even know why I'm here to be honest. I think it was your wedding announcement she threw in my face. It was just so sweet. I had to see what kind of girl would cover her announcement in bright red poppies. And here you are. Just as I pictured you." Cherish sighed as if she were exhausted and scanned the room quickly.

Iris's head swam as she took in the addition of yet another woman Riley had cheated on her with. *Correction.* Still cheating on her with.

"Now, don't faint. I work out, but not enough to catch you and all that lace. Give me your email and I'll forward you Riley's emails. You know, in case you want extra proof. "

Iris sounded like a robot as she gave her information to the woman. Cherish finished adding the address to her phone and then slipped it into her purse.

Cherish winced at Iris's white face and reached out and patted her shoulder. "So you have a choice, I guess. Ignore what I've told you and leave on your honeymoon as if everything's fine, or save yourself a lifetime of heartache. It's up to you. Now, since I've done my good deed for the day, I think I'll head out."

Iris didn't even watch as Cherish walked quickly down the hallway of the reception center and out into the bright summer light.

"Iris! There you are. I've been looking all over for you, dear. It's almost time to cut the cake."

Iris looked up at her mother-in-law, Clarisse Shelton, and shuddered. She glanced over her shoulder at the door leading to freedom, knowing that if she ran for it, it would only make matters worse.

"I'd like you to get Riley for me, please," Iris said in a strained voice. Clarisse's eyes sharpened on her as she noticed Iris's pale, distraught face. She turned without saying a word and hurried back down the hallway toward the ballroom.

Iris sidled down the hallway until she could see all of the people moving about, smiling, dancing, eating, and celebrating. Her parents were dancing together, smiling innocently as they gazed into each other's eyes. Her father looked up, laughing at something her mother had said. She followed Clarisse's frantic search for Riley to a dark corner where Riley was talking to one of her business associates, a stunning redhead from England. Martine Wickman. They looked like they were having a deep, interesting conversation.

Clarisse tapped her son on the shoulder and motioned toward where Iris still stood in the shadows. Riley looked confused but hurried toward her, completely unaware that she knew his secret. He gave her a crooked half smile as he took her cold hand in his.

"You're missing your own party, Iris. Mom said you looked upset and wanted to talk to me. What's up?" Glancing down at his watch, he added, "We've got to get a move on if we're going to make it to the airport in time."

2

She studied his beautiful face and just now noticed how bored he looked. His curly, dark-blond hair always gave him a carefree look, as if he'd just come from a day at the beach. But that wasn't it at all. He was bored to death and he was at his own wedding reception. Now she could understand why.

"I want a divorce." She said the words softly and watched to see if he would be shocked or upset. His calm, unruffled personality had always attracted her. But now she knew that she had been wrong. He wasn't composed; he was completely detached. At least from her.

Riley sighed and leaned up against the wall. Crossing his arms across his chest, he finally looked her in the eyes. "What? Just because I was flirting a little bit with Martine? Oh, please. Can we cut the possessive wife act until we're back from our honeymoon?"

Iris glanced over his shoulder at Martine, who had joined a circle of friends. Even as she laughed and talked, her eyes remained glued to Riley's back. It dawned on Iris that just because she knew about two women Riley had relationships with didn't mean they were the only two.

"I've just been talking to Cherish. Gorgeous blonde. You two are so close, she was a little sad that she hadn't gotten an invitation to your wedding," she said, finally gaining Riley's complete attention. He stood up stiffly and turned his head, looking for her.

"You just missed her." Iris noted the sudden color on Riley's cheeks. She'd finally cracked his boredom.

Riley cleared his throat and glanced over his shoulder at the party going on behind him. "I can explain everything, I promise. Let's just get through this and then we'll talk, okay? Don't ruin this for our families, Iris. You know how long my mom's wanted us to get married. If you throw a little temper tantrum and ruin our reception, you'll break her heart. Just put a big smile on, let's go cut the cake, and then we'll get out of here. Just you and me. We'll work through this, I promise. And just for the record, Cherish is a liar. She's been after me from the first day I met her. You know how girls like her are." He looked her square in the eyes. "I promise you, I've been completely faithful to you."

Iris felt like throwing up. "I might actually have believed you, except for the text messages she showed me. Also, you might want to watch your back. I hear Germaine's not very happy with you either."

Riley's mouth went slack as she walked past him and through the

3

laughing crowd of people calling out congratulations and patting her on the back. She walked to the stage where the band was and reached for the microphone as if it had been waiting for her. As everyone quieted down, she ignored the beautiful centerpieces and flowers she had picked out, the cake she had helped design, and the hundreds of people who had come to celebrate her marriage to the man of her dreams. She ignored everything and everybody except for her mom and dad. They smiled at her expectantly. She had lived her whole life trying not to disappoint them. Trying to make them proud. She sighed as she felt the last piece of her heart shatter and fall to the bottom of her toes. The tears began to slip gently down her cheeks as she lifted her chin up.

"Can I have everyone's attention please?"

Chapter 1

Sophie Kellen grabbed a can of Fresca and plopped down on the huge, overstuffed lime-green couch next to Maggie. She watched her friends, Allison and Jacie, who were sitting across from her on matching green chairs, laugh and giggle and sighed in contentment. Once a month, sometimes twice if they were bored, they'd meet at Maggie's little art gallery and hang out. No husbands, no kids, no distractions. They'd eat salty, sugary, naughty food, laugh way too much, and relax as only you can with real friends. She loved her husband and her son more than her life, but these three women kept her sane.

Tonight there was a purpose to their get-together, though. Well, at least Sophie had a purpose. Her husband Sam's younger brother Trey was turning into someone she didn't know anymore. Her carefree, flirty, confident brother-in-law had turned into a bitter cynic she didn't recognize. It wasn't really his fault. He just kept falling for the wrong women. First, Sam's ex-girlfriend, Tess. *What a psycho.* Sophie shuddered at the memory. And then Allison. Sophie glanced at Allison but couldn't stop smiling. Allison and her new husband, Will, were perfect for each other. Trey was still having a hard time understanding that. Who could blame him, though? Allison was gorgeous. Long, blonde hair, killer eyes, and a great personality.

Sophie blew a strand of red, curly hair out of her eyes. Trey just needed help. It was like he thought life was over. If he couldn't have who he wanted, then he didn't want anyone. Yep, it was time to step in and fix Trey.

"I swear Trey hates women," she complained.

"Uh, that would be my fault," Allison said guiltily.

Jacie nodded her head in complete agreement. "I think you and Tess have ruined him for life. Last week, when I was trimming his hair, Carsyn, our cute little receptionist, offered to get him a drink, and he said no. He didn't even smile at her. He was so not interested in her, she could have been me."

Allison squirmed in her chair. "He didn't even try to flirt with her?"

Jacie shook her head. "Nah. He said, 'No, thanks,' and went back to reading *Time* magazine. It was an article about genetic mutations in fish. Seriously."

Allison ran her hands through her long hair and looked truly upset. "We have to do something. I can't be completely happy when I know Trey is miserable because of me. I feel so bad about what happened." As she spoke, she twisted a large diamond around her ring finger.

Sophie grinned at her friend, thankful for the perfect opening. "Allison, you're brilliant. Let's do it. Trey will be our next service project. Jacie, you can plan it all out. I'll come up with the girl. Maggie, you and Luke can double-date with Trey and help things along. You'll be the spy. And, Allison, . . . um, you just stay out of the way. Okay?"

Maggie laughed and picked up the bowl of guacamole. "No way. *I'll* come up with the girl, and *you* be the spy. Why would I want to double with Trey when I can be at home with my gorgeous husband and son?"

Sophie frowned, tapping her bright red fingernails against her soda can. "But I already have a girl in mind and you're funny and super easy to be around. Trey needs you, Maggie. You're like human guacamole. You go with everything."

Jacie snorted and got off her chair to snag the bowl of guacamole from Maggie's lap. "Share," she ordered as she set the bowl back on the table. "Now that that's settled, let's talk strategy."

Maggie glared at Jacie. "I was hungry." She pulled her feet up onto the couch and added, "And no strategy yet. If anyone was listening, you would already know that I have this in the bag. I know the perfect girl for Trey," she said with a satisfied, cocky smile. Flipping her long, wavy brown hair over her shoulder, Maggie opened up a bag of gluten-free pretzels.

Sophie crinkled up her nose and shot her friend a competitive look. "But I already have the perfect girl for Trey."

Jacie looked back and forth between Sophie and Maggie, a devilish look creeping across her face. "Okay, now this is getting interesting. Let's make it a little contest, shall we? If Trey falls in love with Sophie's girl, she wins. If Trey goes for your girl, Maggie, you win."

Allison put her skittles down, looking uncomfortable. She held up her hand. "If Trey could hear you guys talking, he'd be furious. This is wrong. Yeah, set him up on a couple blind dates. No big deal. But a contest? No way."

Sophie and Maggie ignored Allison and stared at each other.

"Free salon services for a year," Maggie said, raising an eyebrow.

"A portrait of me on a horse, with a sunset and a few strategically placed leaves," Sophie said with a straight face.

All four women burst out laughing. Maggie ended up on the floor and Jacie had to pound Allison on the back as a Skittle went down the wrong way.

"How about a portrait of Adam with his new puppy instead?" Maggie said when she could breathe again.

Sophie blew a red ringlet out of her eyes and sighed happily. "Fine. But Sam will be very disappointed."

Allison wiped the tears from her eyes and leaned tiredly against the arm of the chair. "Seriously? You're really going to do this?"

Sophie and Maggie nodded in complete agreement.

"Why not?" Jacie said, trying to sound innocent. "You have to ask yourself, if you're not actively trying to help someone, are you really a Christian?"

Allison rolled her eyes. "Fine, but if I feel this is getting out of hand, I should have the right to stop it. I feel responsible for Trey, and I don't want to hurt him any more than he has been."

Sophie stopped grinning and looked serious. "No one is going to hurt Trey. He's Sam's little brother. I love him more than all of you guys put together. Trust me, we're not doing this maliciously. We're just going to help him. I mean, look at the poor guy. All he has are Luke and Sam and a couple other college friends. They don't know how to help him. They think golfing is the answer." She looked disgusted.

Maggie, Jacie, and Allison nodded sadly in complete agreement.

"Face it, Allison. We have the skills to do this. If we don't, who knows how long Trey will be locked in his little castle of ice. Frozen in

7

time. Not loving. Not being loved. Not living," Jacie said dramatically.

Allison shook her head and bit her bottom lip. "Fine, but show me the girls first. I think we all need to see and approve your choices before we move forward."

Maggie hummed happily and nodded her head. "Not a problem. You first, Sophie."

Sophie shrugged and grabbed Maggie's laptop off the table. "Do you mind?" she asked, not waiting for a response. She pulled up Facebook, typed in a name, and then motioned for everyone to gather around.

"Let me introduce you to Macie Jo Jackson. Former Miss Atlanta and newly hired hairstylist. She's amazing at highlights. She'll be taking over a lot of my clients so I can spend more time at home. Isn't she gorgeous?"

Maggie's confident smile went down a few watts. "Dang. She's pretty. Look how even her features are. Has she had plastic surgery?"

Sophie frowned and squinted at the picture. "Jacie was going to ask her last week and lost the nerve. We suspect that it's a possibility, but we're going to assume she hasn't for the time being. Everyone loves her to death. She says 'y'all' a lot."

Allison leaned in and frowned at the beautiful girl. "She looks too much like me. Don't you think Trey needs to be with someone different? Someone who doesn't constantly remind him of someone who hurt him?"

Jacie and Sophie looked at each other and considered. Sophie shrugged and clicked through Macie's information. "Some men have a certain type of girl they're attracted to. Trey has always gone for tall blondes. I don't see that changing."

Maggie cleared her throat loudly. "Actually, I agree with Allie. Now put Miss Macie away and get ready to see the woman who will steal Trey Kellen's heart."

Sophie pushed the laptop toward Maggie and waited expectantly. Maggie shook her head and shut the laptop. "Uh-uh. I've got something better. She's Luke's cousin from Washington, and I used her as a model when we were up visiting his aunt and uncle last year."

Sophie, Jacie, and Allison watched as Maggie ran up the stairs to the loft. A few minutes later, she reappeared with a medium-sized picture frame in her hands, looking excited.

Sophie put her quesadilla down and wiped her hands on a napkin.

"Fine, show us your girl. No way can she be better than Macie Jo, though."

Maggie stuck her tongue out and slowly turned the picture around to face the three women. Jacie was the first to break the silence.

"Wow."

Sophie cleared her throat and walked closer to see the picture better. "But you're an artist. You can make anyone look like some Renaissance work of art. You're better than airbrushing," she said dismissively.

Allison pushed Sophie out of the way and leaned in closer to see the woman leaning on a tree and looking over her shoulders as if she'd just been caught playing hide-and-seek. Simple joy and innocent beauty glowed in her eyes.

"But her hair is so dark. It's darker than yours, Maggie," Sophie said shaking her head.

Maggie smiled contentedly. "I know. Think Cherry Coke. It's gorgeous, and her eyes, I'm not kidding, celery green. The most beautiful, clear green you could ever imagine."

Allison sighed happily. "I like her, Maggie. When can we meet her?"

Maggie turned and gently leaned the picture up against the wall before sitting back down on the couch. "Well, you see, there's a little issue."

Sophie bounced on the couch and hooted. "See! I knew it. She might be the most beautiful woman in the world, but there's an issue. Get your paints ready, Maggie, because I want that picture done by Christmas."

Maggie glared at Sophie and realized she really did want a year's worth of salon services. And bragging rights of course. She decided to edit a few things before she continued.

"Um, well the issue is that she isn't here yet. She's not getting into town until next week sometime." Grabbing the last quesadilla from the coffee table, she collapsed onto the couch.

"Oh, I thought you were going to say she already had a boyfriend or something," Sophie said with a laugh.

Maggie looked guiltily down at her feet as she swallowed her bite. "Yeah, that would be a huge issue, huh?" She looked everywhere but at her friends.

Jacie looked at her suspiciously but let it go. "We've got our two contenders for Trey's heart. We have the prizes selected. Now, we talk rules. Rule number one is, whoever Trey goes for, we all support. No sabotaging each other for the sake of highlights or free pictures of your kid. This is about Trey. This is about helping Trey heal and move on to a healthy, loving relationship. Right?"

Sophie and Maggie looked offended, and both of them started talking at the same time.

Allison held up her hands for quiet. "Jacie is right. No getting crazy competitive. We help out when we can. We push people in the right direction, but in the end, it's about Trey picking the woman *he* wants. Not who *we* want."

All four women agreed and went back to eating. After a few minutes, Sophie looked up. "Wait a second. What about the other rules?"

Jacie laughed. "There's only one rule."

Sophie and Maggie nodded and punched their fists and pointed at each other as if they were in a prize-fighting ring.

"Game on, Maggie," Sophie said with a sneer.

Maggie raised her eyebrows and flexed her arms. "You mean game over. I've already won."

Jacie and Allison laughed and threw pillows at both of their friends. The salsa ended up on Maggie's carpet, and the guacamole got spiked with Fresca, but the night ended with a lot of laughter and excitement.

* * *

After everyone left, Maggie flopped on her couch and sighed. Her contender for Trey's heart didn't have a little issue. She had a *huge* issue. She had an ex-husband and she was moving to Alpine to start over. Trey wouldn't mind, though. Maggie closed her eyes and leaned her head back, staring at the ceiling. *Nah*. It wouldn't be a big deal.

Chapter 2

ris set a box down and walked over to look out the front window of the house she was renting. Luke had told her over the phone that it was an older house and kind of small. He hadn't been exaggerating. It was nothing like her glitzy condo in Seattle overlooking Puget Sound. She sighed heavily as she watched her cousin and his wife, Maggie, lift boxes out of the back of her dad's truck. She was happy to have the help, but they were so . . . *nice*. So smiley. They were probably going to invite her over for dinner. A lot.

She leaned her head against the cool glass and closed her eyes. She just wanted to disappear for a little while. She didn't want to be Iris Levine anymore. She didn't want anyone's compassion or pity or sympathy. But more than anything, she didn't want to be the object of anyone's gossip.

Iris turned and walked into the small kitchen, grimacing at the Formica countertops and outdated appliances. Here she was, one of the best interior designers from her company, and this was the environment she had chosen to surround herself with. Her old boss, David Winters, would laugh himself sick. But what David didn't know, wouldn't hurt her.

"There you are," Maggie said. Oh, you must be exhausted. Luke put the last box in the garage for you. Why don't you take a nap and then come over for dinner around five? Don't even think about unpacking until tomorrow," Maggie said, her blue eyes glowing with concern.

Iris tried to smile back. It must have looked ghastly because

Maggie's eyes sharpened in worry. Pumping up her smile a few notches, Iris showed teeth this time.

"That is so kind of you, Maggie, but honestly, I think I'll just fall in bed and sleep until tomorrow. I appreciate the invitation to dinner, but . . ." She let her sentence trail off as she gazed past Maggie's shoulder, thinking about when she might actually be interested in socializing. She had no idea.

Maggie nodded her head as if she could read Iris's mind. "Oh, no worries. When you're feeling up to it, we'll ask again. I left a few things in the fridge in case you get hungry and don't want to run to the store yet. My number's on the fridge. Call me for anything, okay?"

Iris tried to smile again but gave up halfway through. Maggie nodded grimly and then turned to leave. Iris heard the door shut gently and leaned against the counter. Finally. Alone. Exactly what she wanted. Why else would she leave her dream job, her family and friends, and her home to come to a little podunk town like Alpine? There was nothing here. No shopping, no restaurants, nothing but houses, a couple schools, churches, and mountains. A person could disappear here and no one would even notice.

She sighed at the phone number on the fridge. If Maggie and Luke got too nosey, she'd just move again. Guatemala maybe.

Iris pondered world geography as she dragged herself up the stairs to where Maggie had made her bed with fresh sheets. Not even bothering to take off her shoes, she collapsed on the bed. *Aaaaaahhhhhh. Silence.* Iris closed her eyes and smiled for the first time in two months.

* * *

Maggie followed Luke back to their house and shut the door firmly behind her. She let Luke pay the babysitter while she checked on her son, Talon, who was taking a nap in his crib. Afterward, she wandered into the kitchen. Luke found her a moment later, tapping her foot and staring off into space.

"Hey now, don't be disappointed. You said yourself she was exhausted. This just means there'll be more fajitas for us," Luke said, smiling cheerfully.

Maggie shook her head. "No, Luke, it's more than exhausted. You know how I can read people. Her eyes were so bleak. It was like looking at a ghost. There was too much pain. She's not the same woman I met last year."

Luke frowned and walked over to his wife. "Sweetie, now come on. She just drove twelve hours from Washington. She's emotionally and physically exhausted. Let's give her a little space and time. She'll bounce back, you'll see." Maggie didn't look convinced. "You don't know Iris like I do. This girl is a winner. She dives into life. She's one of those people who is driven to succeed; she's been top of her class in everything. She's only twenty-four years old and she's practically the top in her field. She glows with ambition. To be honest, it's actually kind of intimidating. There's no way a girl like that just gives up because some guy broke her heart. I promise you."

Maggie sighed and wrapped her arms around her husband's waist, leaning her head on his shoulder. "But her eyes said something different, Luke. I'm worried." She hesitated for a moment before adding, "And I've promised all the girls that I would set Iris up with Trey, but from where I'm standing, there's no way that's going to happen."

Luke laughed and kissed the top of Maggie's head. "Actually, I think that's brilliant. Trey's just the man to make her forget about Riley. Man, what a loser. He had a girl like Iris and didn't even appreciate it. Total idiot. I'll see what I can do on Trey's end."

Maggie pulled back and shook her head. "No, Luke. No blind dates. If either one of them thinks we're setting them up, it'll ruin everything. Plus, it's just way too early for Iris. She'd probably stab anyone who mentioned men or dating."

Luke looked skeptical but shrugged. "Fine, no blind dates. I hated those too. Just leave everything to me. I'm so good they'll never know what hit them," he said as he opened the fridge and took out the steak for the fajitas.

Maggie's face broke into a smile as she sat down at her counter. "Luke, have I ever mentioned how attractive a strong, confident, and efficient man is?"

Luke grinned and started slicing the steak. "Only every day."

Maggie laughed and leaned her chin on her hands. "So what's your plan?"

Luke expertly cut the meat into thin slices. "You've seen that new project on Main Street, right? Some new restaurant with modern cuisine, blah, blah, blah. Well, Sam's company was hired to build it, and Trey is the project manager. Coincidently, Iris is the best interior decorator I know of. I'll just mention to Sam how my cousin has just moved here. Mention a few of her credentials and the jobs she's done. Maybe let slip how she's won a few prestigious awards. I'll tell him how busy she is, but since I'm his close friend, I might be able to convince her to take on the job. I'll seem a little unsure, but since it's a tiny project, maybe, *just maybe,* they could get her."

Maggie jumped off the stool and rushed around the counter to hug her husband from behind. "You're the best. And you're all mine," she said with relish.

Luke grinned happily. "And don't you ever, ever forget it."

Maggie felt her excitement return full force. As much as she liked Trey, her main concern was Iris now. She wanted to see that bleakness replaced with joy. And what better way to do that than a new love and a new life.

Chapter 3

Iris slept for the next three days. She got up to eat and take care of the necessities of life, but then she found herself back in bed almost immediately. On the fourth day, she woke and stretched, knowing that she really did have to go on with life. Riley would probably love the idea of her languishing in bed, miserable and depressed, and to be honest, she was. But she wasn't the type to stay down forever. Three days was perfect.

She showered and ate the last of the cereal Maggie had given her. Today she'd have to go shopping and exploring. She looked through her clothes and frowned. She didn't feel like wearing a pantsuit. She didn't feel like wearing her expensive jeans and cashmere sweaters either. All of her clothes had been picked to portray who she wanted to express to the world: a successful, classy, and fashionable modern woman. But she didn't want to be that right now. Who would care? She didn't. She flopped down on her bed and covered her eyes with her arm. She wanted to dress how she felt. She was angry and bitter, and she felt like breaking things a lot lately.

Iris grinned as she thought about going for a biker chick look. Her parents would be shocked. Riley wouldn't believe it, that's for sure. Iris smiled at the thought and sat up. Why not? Who would know? Who would care? No one knew her here. Well, except Luke of course, but he was a busy family man. He probably wouldn't even notice. She could totally remake herself. At least for a little while. It would be like going on vacation. A vacation from reality.

Iris felt a little weight fall off her shoulders as she flung on a pair of jeans and grabbed a cream-colored cashmere sweater. She had to wear something to go to the mall.

Iris spent the next three hours combing the mall for just the right look. She was an expert on decorating houses and businesses. Now she was going to decorate herself. And when she started a project, she was meticulous.

She started with the basics. Black. And since money wasn't an issue, she spent quite a bit on a slick black leather jacket. It was tough and mean, and it suited her mood perfectly. As she shopped, Iris wondered if she should go the whole way and buy a motorcycle. She decided to put it on the agenda. A test drive couldn't hurt.

Eager to switch to her new look, Iris changed in the bathroom at the mall. She checked herself out in the full-length mirror and sighed happily. The low-slung distressed jeans with their fading and holes made her giggle. She had to admit the silk-screen black shirt with the phoenix was impressive artistically but still not something she would have ever chosen to wear. But she did love the boots. She'd never worn a pair of biker boots in her life, but now she wasn't sure why. They were gorgeous. The heels made her five-foot-seven frame two inches taller while giving her a sense of power. If she did come across Riley, she'd be able to put a few boot prints on his rear.

Iris frowned in the mirror. Her face and hair looked the same. She wanted a full transformation. Her long, dark-auburn hair that fell to the middle of her back looked perfect. But she didn't want perfect anymore. She wanted mean, dark, and dangerous. She wasn't quite done.

Iris threw her shopping bags in the back of the truck she had borrowed from her dad for the trip and headed back toward Alpine. On her way to the mall, she had noticed a salon on Main Street. She was used to paying hundreds of dollars for her hair. Jason, her hairstylist for the past four years, would kill her if he knew what she was contemplating. But no one would ever know. Especially not Jason.

Iris turned the radio to a rock station and turned it up until it was painfully loud. Something she would have never done before. She felt her spirits soar as AC/DC screamed about being "Back in Black." Perfect. She couldn't have said it better herself.

She parked in front of the quaint little salon twenty minutes later and breezed through the front doors with a smile on her face. The cute little redhead sitting at the front desk looked up and did a double take. Good. She was probably thinking how tough Iris looked. Iris smiled kindly, not wanting to scare anyone . . . *yet.*

Chapter 4

would like to get my hair, makeup, and nails done. And if you do those cool henna tattoos that last a month, I want a few of those too," the beautiful and slightly crazed-looking woman said with glee.

Sophie Kellen's jaw dropped slightly as she recognized Maggie's girl, Iris. She was right; she'd never seen green eyes quite so clear and so light a green. And those eyes were filled with an unholy fire. She wasn't anything like what Sophie had pictured. She looked like she had just walked out of a New York model shoot for the rich and deadly.

"Wow, your boots are incredible," Sophie said, staring at the toughest footwear she'd seen in years. And she had been to a rodeo just last month.

Iris grinned in delight. "Amazing, aren't they? And worth every penny. So, do you have an opening today or should I come back?"

Sophie cleared her throat and glanced down at the appointment book in front of her. "We can fit you in right now. I can do your hair, and Jacie can do your makeup and nails. We don't do henna tattoos here, but I know a local girl who's amazing at it. Her name's Brittany. She did an Indian bridal design on my arm last year before I went to Lake Powell and I loved it."

Iris nodded her head. "Sounds great. But I don't want anything to do with bridal designs. *Gag.* I want something like a dragon across my back or chains wrapped around my arm. Something like that."

Sophie's eyes widened in alarm. This was who Maggie thought was perfect for Trey? Was she insane?

"Okaaaay, so follow me back and we'll get started."

Iris practically skipped for the chair. She carefully and almost lovingly took off her new leather jacket and draped it on an empty chair beside hers.

Sophie eyed the leather jacket as she put on her apron. "So tell me what you had in mind? Your hair looks amazing. So healthy. I've never actually seen color like this before. Beautiful." As she talked she ran her fingers through the silky strands of Iris's hair.

Iris shrugged and grimaced. "Yeah, but I want something different."

Sophie blinked in surprise. "But this *is* different. No one I know has hair like this. Women everywhere would probably like to kill for your hair."

Iris looked intrigued by the idea but shook her head. "So did you see Katy Perry's hair at the VMA awards?"

Sophie shook her head. "Uh, no. I must have missed that."

Iris grinned. "Me too! But I saw a picture of her at the mall today, and I know what I want. I've always had the natural red highlights, but I want the tips of my hair dark, dark red. Like my hair is turning into fire. And I want the cut to be kind of jagged on the bottom. Think rock star meets anime."

Sophie bit her lip and felt ill at the thought of putting chemicals on such gorgeous hair.

"Hey, Sophie! I'm back from lunch. I can take over if you need to run."

Sophie turned around in relief to see Macie Jo, the new stylist and her pick for Trey. She felt a little calmer as she contrasted the two women. There was nothing to worry about. Trey would never go for some crazy woman with rock star hair. She could just see the portrait of Adam now.

"Actually, that would be perfect. Do you mind if I hand you over to Macie Jo? She's our newest stylist. Everyone loves her, and she's very talented."

Iris studied the blonde standing behind her and shrugged. She didn't care who did her hair as long as she got what she wanted.

Sophie waved good-bye and left quickly out the back. She couldn't watch the desecration of something so beautiful. It made her slightly ill to think of it. Plus, she needed to talk to Jacie, Allison, and Maggie—*especially Maggie*. What in the world had she been thinking?

Chapter 5

I ris smiled happily as she walked through the aisles of the grocery store. She flipped her hair over her shoulder and couldn't help grinning. Macie Jo was a genius. She'd bleached the tips of her hair out and then added the dark red. Macie insisted that was the only way to get the color she wanted since her hair was so dark and healthy. It had taken longer than she had planned, but in the end, the result was what mattered. The jagged cut went perfectly with the flame theme. Macie had been thrilled with the tip she had left her and had promised to do a touch-up if the color washed out too quickly.

Iris glanced in her shopping cart and frowned at all the junk food she was collecting. Chips, soda, and Hot Pockets. She and Riley had been on a strictly organic diet for the last six months. She smiled as she realized there wasn't one organic thing in her cart. She really was on vacation. Moving on to the ice cream aisle, she glared at the tall man standing right in front of the Ben and Jerry's. She was patient though. She studied her amazing, deadly reflection in the glass doors and nodded her head. She was one tough, strong woman.

The man sensed her presence and turned to look at her over his shoulder. He reminded her a little of that actor Ryan Gosling. Way too cute for his own good. His eyes widened a little, but he didn't look scared or nervous. Iris frowned. She'd have to practice looking mean in the mirror when she got home. The man smiled at her as if he were a giant Ken doll and held up two cartons of ice cream.

"What sounds better? Chunky Monkey or Late Night Snack?"

Iris was surprised he was trying to engage her in conversation. She had gone to great lengths to put an invisible *STAY AWAY* sign on her forehead. But he was one of those ultra-beautiful men who probably couldn't comprehend a woman not wanting to talk to him. Just like Riley. They actually looked a tiny bit alike. Except this guy was taller and bulkier, his hair was lighter and sun streaked, and his eyes were light blue, not hazel. His smile was nicer than Riley's too. He'd probably spent a lot of time torturing innocent women with that dangerous smile of his. Actually he was nothing like Riley. But Riley had taught her well. She was on to him. But at the same time, he did have a good question.

Iris walked forward and looked studiously at the two cartons the man held. "You'd have to really love banana-flavored ice cream, chocolate, and walnuts to go for this one. Late Night Snack? Isn't that the chocolate-covered potato chip one?"

The man grinned and read the carton. "That is so weird. Have you tried it?"

Iris nodded sagely and looked at the shelves full of ice cream. "Of course. I wouldn't consider myself a true Ben and Jerry's fan if I didn't try every flavor they came out with."

The man put the Chunky Monkey back and put the Late Night Snack ice cream in his cart. "Well, now I'm intrigued. What flavor does a serious fan go for?"

Iris scanned the shelves and sighed happily as she snagged the Chunky Monkey he had just put back. "And to think this is the last one," she said. She gave him her nastiest grin as she put the beloved ice cream in her cart and walked away.

"Hey! You just played me," the man yelled, following quickly after her.

Iris grinned wickedly. Had he not seen the boots? Honestly, this guy was not good at reading the cues she was sending out. He caught up with her and grabbed her cart forcing her to stop.

"So since you just stole my ice cream right out from under me, I think you should at least introduce yourself. Obviously you're new in town. My name is Trey Kellen. What's yours?" He smiled at her cautiously.

Iris looked up at Trey. Geez, what was he, six three? "You're right, you got played. But you really should thank me. Everyone should try that flavor at least once. It's not that bad. Not as good as Chunky Monkey, of course, but that's life for you. Kind of unfair. And you're right. I am new in town. I'm Iris, Luke Petersen's cousin. I just got into town a few days ago."

Trey leaned up against a freezer door and crossed his arms. "Now that's interesting. Luke happens to be one of my best friends, and not once did he mention to me that his cousin was coming to town."

Iris shrugged and studied her newly painted fingernails. Vampire black. She smiled happily at the high gloss. Her nails were definitely rated PG-13 at the very least. "Well, he probably knows that I'm just here to kind of blend in. You know, be anonymous. No big splash."

Trey laughed at her and did a quick glance over, pausing on her hair. "Yeah, I don't think you're going to be anonymous. You're kind of, um . . . different from a lot of the girls who live around here."

Iris looked up and grinned at Trey. "Seriously? That's exactly what I was going for."

Trey tilted his head as if he was trying to figure her out. "So why'd you come to Alpine? Job, family, . . . *relationship*?"

Iris sighed heavily, all happiness draining from her eyes. "No, no, and *no*. Definitely no men. So be sure and tell all the single men that they're safe from me. I am now an official man-free zone."

Trey laughed and shook his head. "Oh, my."

Iris glared at him and put her hands on her hips. "Excuse me? What is that supposed to mean? Not every woman is out to get a guy, or get married, or be in a relationship or, or . . . anything!" she finished rather lamely.

Trey stepped back, holding his hands up defensively. "Please don't hurt me. Your boots are intimidating enough. I only said, 'oh, my,' because I'm with you. I'm an official woman-free zone."

"Really?"

"Yes. You're actually standing a little too close to be honest. I'm getting a little uncomfortable."

Iris noticed she was standing quite close and blushed, stepping back quickly. "Oh, sorry. But, wow."

Trey nodded sadly. "I'm done with women. Burned one too many times."

Iris patted his arm sympathetically. "Me too. Except I was never burned before. I just had one big bonfire. But it was enough."

Trey's light blue eyes lost their teasing glint and turned sympathetic. "Well, since we're both off the market, at least we're safe with each other, right?"

Iris crinkled her nose and considered. "I guess. But really, I hate men right now. I don't think you're safe around me. I could accidently hurt you just because you're, you know, a good-looking guy." She inched farther away.

Trey smiled at the good looking reference and reached out to touch a strand of her red tipped hair. "Well, we'd have to have rules—safety parameters—if we ever hung out. But you're right, I don't think I could take getting kicked around by someone who owns a Harley."

Iris grinned at him. "I'm going to get one. I can't wait."

Trey laughed as they walked toward the checkout stand. He even helped her put her groceries on the conveyor belt as he offered suggestions on where to go to test-drive motorcycles.

Iris was even prepared to admit that Trey might be one of the few nice guys left in the world, until she started putting her groceries away when she got home. Reaching for the Chunky Monkey ice cream she'd bought, she ended up grabbing Late Night Snack instead. He switched the cartons. He'd played her!

Iris growled and knew that if he were standing anywhere close by, she would have gladly kicked the tar out of him. She hated men.

Chapter 6

Trey grinned as he leaned back in his black leather recliner and turned to ESPN on his flat screen. He dipped his spoon in the ice cream carton and took a huge bite. The Chunky Monkey actually tasted better knowing that he had swiped it from right under the nose of Iris of the wild hair. Wild everything actually. She looked like some poor lost model trying on clothes for Halloween. Not that she didn't look good. She did, if you went for women who lived on the edge. But he wasn't buying it. She was having too much fun stomping around in her boots to be legit. And all that talk about being a "man-free zone." She must have been dragged through the dirt by some serious loser to announce something like that.

Trey clicked through a few stations before he landed back on ESPN and took another huge bite. He had been kidding about being his own woman-free zone. For the most part, he loved women. He just had the world's worst luck with them. He enjoyed them, he liked being with them, he loved dating them. But every time he actually fell in love, disaster. Sam's ex, Tess: biggest disaster ever. And then there was Allison. Trey shook his head and tried to put his memory of her out of his head. She'd really gotten to him. It had been love at first sight for him. And in the end, she had basically just been using him to make Will jealous.

His fists clenched at the thought of Will. He knew in his heart that he would be a happier man if he could just break a few of Will's bones. Not many, just the ones in his face.

Trey counted to ten and tried to relax. The one woman he wanted, and Will took her from him. And there wasn't one thing he could do about it. They'd been blissfully married for six months now. You'd think he could get over it. But he wasn't. He snarled at everybody. He down-right hated Will. And he wasn't pleased with women at the moment. He even stole ice cream from brokenhearted women at the grocery store. And enjoyed doing it.

Trey smiled and shook his head. Talking to Iris had actually cheered him up more than anything else had in a long time. Poor thing. She was probably staring at her carton of junky potato chip ice cream and wringing her hands right now. He laughed at the thought but groaned immediately as he heard the doorbell. If it was Sam or Luke coming over to take him golfing one more time, he'd have to make up a sprained ankle or something.

He padded barefoot through the house he had bought two months before and opened the front door. Not Sam. *Close.* Sophie.

"Hey, gorgeous. How's my beautiful sister-in-law?" he said hugging her automatically. Opening the door wide, he let her and his little nephew, Adam, walk in.

He leaned over and picked up Adam and threw his nephew in the air, making him giggle and squeal. Trey laughed and felt his heart lighten at the sight. Adam looked like a miniature of Sam, his older brother. Which meant that if he ever had a kid, he'd look a lot like this one. The thought made his heart ache as he gently lowered the little boy and shut the door.

"Sorry for barging in on you," Sophie said, "but I had some left-over Ravioli and thought you might be hungry." She walked into Trey's kitchen and set the casserole dish on the counter. Turning, she smiled brightly at him. *Too* brightly.

Trey frowned. She was up to something. "Well thank you, Sophie. You know I'm always hungry."

He obediently grabbed a fork out of the drawer and opened the lid, letting some of the steam escape. He munched on a few bites as Sophie did an inventory of the kitchen. He hadn't cooked one thing lately, so hopefully it would pass the inspection.

"Remember how I told everyone I was thinking of spending more time at home?"

Trey nodded absently and speared another ravioli, waiting for Sophie to get to the point of her visit.

"Well, I found the most amazing stylist ever. She started this week, and I have to admit I'm a little jealous. She's taking over my clients, and they all seem to love her," she said, grabbing a fork and taking a bite herself as Adam pulled all the pots and pans out of the cabinets.

"Sophie, no one could take your place. As a matter of fact, I refuse to let anyone else touch my hair but you," Trey promised, wondering if Sophie could actually hear Adam banging the pots on his tile floor with all the strength of a three-year-old.

"Oh, I don't know, Trey. When you meet Macie Jo, you're going to want her to do your hair," Sophie said casually as she bent and removed the pot from Adam's fist, replacing it a moment later with a sucker from her purse.

As another forkful of ravioli was midway to his mouth, Trey paused as he finally got the reason for Sophie's visit. She was trying to set him up. It seemed like everybody in Alpine was determined to set him up with the perfect woman. He got two or three calls a week minimum. He set the fork down and stood up to his full height, towering over his beautiful but short sister-in-law.

Sophie swallowed nervously and quickly took a picture out of her purse and shoved it into Trey's hands.

"Just take a look, Trey. She's perfect. She's beautiful. And she's the sweetest girl I've ever met," she pleaded.

Trey lifted up the picture to judge for himself. She wasn't kidding. The woman was beautiful. Big blue eyes. Lots and lots of blonde hair. Brilliant white smile. He sighed and lowered the picture to the counter. She reminded him of Allison, and that just depressed him.

"Sophie, now that is one gorgeous woman," he said, shaking his head with regret.

Sophie's eyes lit up. "She is! She was Miss Atlanta. I'm not even kidding. She won a pageant. And she has a southern accent. You'll love it, Trey. She calls everyone 'honey,'" Sophie said in delight.

Trey winced, knowing that he didn't want to be called "honey." Sophie had to be stopped. He'd rather have his chest waxed than be set up with an ex-pageant queen.

"Sophie, if you had just been here a day earlier. Wow, I'm almost

27

regretting this now." He picked up the picture to look at it longingly one last time so Sophie would know how much he appreciated her efforts.

Sophie frowned. "Regret what?" she said, snatching the picture out of his hands, looking for any faults or failings.

Trey sighed loudly and took another bite of ravioli. It was actually pretty decent. "Um, well, you see, I just met a woman. You'll love her, Sophie. She's tall, gorgeous, and super sweet. If I hadn't met her first, I would have loved to go out with this beauty here. But you know I'm a one-woman kind of man. When I'm focused on one woman, I can't even think of anyone else," he said honestly.

Sophie's face crumpled, and she threw her arms around Trey's neck, giving him a hard hug. "Oh, Trey. I know, sweetie. That's why I've been so worried about you. You're the sweetest, most loving man in the world, and you deserve to have someone who will love you back just as much you love her," she said, tearing up.

Trey swallowed and felt queasy at the pity he saw in her eyes. Yeah, that did it. Iris would have to be sacrificed for his greater good.

"I know, Sophie. I know. That's why I feel like the luckiest man alive. To think that I could deserve someone as perfect as Iris," he said, reaching for the fork Sophie had knocked out of his hands. He took another bite and then looked up just as Sophie's mouth shut. She looked shocked. No, no that wasn't it. She looked horrified. Trey continued to chew his ravioli as he grinned. Sophie must have already met the one and only Iris. That would be the only explanation for the look of wild horror on her face. He hid a chuckle in his fist as he pretended to cough.

"She's the woman of my dreams, Sophie. She's so different from anyone I've ever dated. It's like she doesn't even care about men or what she looks like or what other people think of her. I have to admit, she's a breath of fresh air."

Sophie nodded her head silently as she struggled to find something to say. Trey decided to give her a few more minutes. "And her hair. I don't know where she gets her hair done, but when I saw her hair, I knew this was the girl for me. It was like silk-dipped flames. Art, Sophie. It was hair art. And her natural hair color, I can't even describe it. It's the most amazing color I've ever seen. It's . . ." Trey paused. He really didn't know how to describe it.

"It's Cherry Coke," Sophie whispered, picking Adam off the floor and hugging him to her side.

Trey grinned and picked a piece of fuzz off of Adam's sucker before he stuck it back in his mouth. "That's it. Cherry Coke. She's one of a kind, Sophie. You'll love her. And if I'm lucky, maybe she'll be your sister-in-law someday soon," he said, wondering if that was pushing it too far.

Sophie's mouth was clamped tight into a straight line, and now she looked mad. Trey walked over to the fridge and grabbed a soda can. He grimaced when he noticed he was out of Fresca. He only bought them for her. He silently offered her one of his favorites, but she shook her head automatically.

"Well, okay, then," Sophie said, at a loss for words.

Trey nodded in agreement. "Okay, then."

He walked Sophie to the door, kissed her on the cheek, and got a sticky hug from Adam, who had lost his sucker. He watched them drive away, waving until he couldn't see them anymore. But as he walked back into the house, he couldn't stop the feeling of freedom that was blooming wherever he stepped. Freedom from blind dates. Freedom from pity. Freedom from all the pressure of having the whole stinking town of Alpine know he was madly in love with Allison Carson. Freedom from seeing Will Carson's smirking, stupid face.

Trey stepped over a pot strewn on the kitchen floor and picked up Adam's forgotten sucker. Yeah, this was perfect. He paused as he realized he had forgotten one very important thing: Iris. No way was Sophie going to let this go unless she had proof. Iris would have to be brought in on his little plan. Trey sighed and grabbed a rag to wipe up the floor. He'd have to talk to her again. He shrugged at the thought. Talking to her had been the highlight of his day. She'd go for it. Unless she was mad about the ice cream. Then there might be a problem.

Throwing the rag into the sink, he headed for the garage. He was going on an Iris hunt. He smiled as he looked at his secret weapon. Opening the garage door, he wished Iris could be standing right there with him as the sunlight streamed in on his brand new Ducati Diavel. 162 horsepower. Enough said. There was no way she could withstand that kind of power. He threw on his helmet and revved the engine, feeling better and better. One ride on this baby and she'd be putty in his hands.

Chapter 7

Iris was sitting on her front porch with her boots up on the railing, eating straight from the carton of Late Night Snack and imagining herself doing some incredibly complex karate moves on Trey Kellen. Then her daydream switched to Riley getting his rear end handed to him. He would take one look at her new black boots and awe-inspiring hair and realize that there would be no mercy for him. He probably wouldn't even take it like a man either. She grinned as she pictured him crying on his knees. Begging for mercy.

Iris dropped the spoon and lowered her boots to the porch when she first heard, then saw, the most beautiful motorcycle drive up to Luke's house next door. She sat up straighter as a guy hopped off the motorcycle and sauntered up to the door, taking off his skull-emblazoned helmet. Iris had never felt so jealous in her life. She stared at the motorcycle and wondered if the guy would mind if she had a closer look. She stood up, still holding her ice cream, and leaned on the porch railing, trying to see if the guy had walked in the house or if he was still outside. Luke's porch was in shadow, so it was hard to see what was going on, but she could just make out Luke pointing right at her.

Iris blinked as the man turned and looked at her, then waved his thanks to Luke and headed down the steps toward her. Iris swallowed nervously. She was new to the whole "I'm tougher than nails and meaner than a prison guard" persona, so her old self backed up a foot. Until she saw the man's face. Her face hardened automatically, and she sat back down, resting her feet back on the porch railing. She took another bite of ice cream so he would know she was completely unimpressed with him and his motorcycle. She glared, unblinking, at him as he made his way up the stairs.

"Well, now that looks delicious. I was so disappointed when I got home and realized that our cartons accidently got mixed up. I had to find you immediately and apologize. I am so sorry, Iris. I remembered you mentioning that Luke was your cousin, so I hurried over here as fast as I could," he said, sounding apologetic and sincere.

Iris snorted and rolled her eyes. The laughter in his eyes was a huge giveaway. He was totally lying. She took another bite of ice cream and pretended he wasn't there. She stared around him at Luke's house and smiled as she noticed that Luke and Maggie had decided to spend some time out on their own front porch. *Nosy neighbors.*

Trey cleared his throat and handed her a small brown bag. Iris took the bag automatically and glanced inside. A brand-new carton of Chunky Monkey. *Hmmm.* Was there a possibility that he wasn't lying? No. So what was really going on? She set the bag down and sighed.

"You rotten jerk. Pretending like you didn't steal my ice cream. What do you want?" She wanted him to know that he hadn't fooled her.

Trey grinned. "Now, I'm not admitting anything, but hypothetically, if I did steal your ice cream, don't you think you deserved it since you manipulated me out of my first choice? And since I already ate your Chunky Monkey, I had to run all the way to Smith's to get this for you. It would be impolite not to forgive me."

Iris licked her spoon and studied Trey, who was standing in the soft September light. He really was gorgeous. And so sure that she would buy whatever it was he was selling. He was probably used to girls throwing themselves at him constantly. She couldn't help glancing at his motorcycle though. What she wouldn't give for a ride on that.

"Yeah, that's not going to happen. I'm not really in the forgiving mood at the moment. I have too many potato chips stuck in my teeth."

Trey laughed and sat down next to her, not waiting for an invitation. "You do crack me up, Iris. You're not like any woman I've ever known."

Iris smiled. Now that was a compliment she would take and enjoy. And it had actually sounded sincere. Something she wasn't sure happened a lot with Trey. "So what is it that you really want, just out of curiosity?" She used the spoon to dig for the last bite of ice cream.

Trey sighed loudly and tilted his head back, pausing as if consider-ing what to say. Iris smiled. He was trying to figure out whether to tell her the truth or to feed her a line. She hoped he would just tell her the truth but was betting on getting a line.

"I would like to bribe you," Trey said, still looking at the roof of her porch.

Iris smiled happily. He had decided on the truth. Wonderful. "I hope that motorcycle has something to do with the bribe," she said, pointing toward the bike with her spoon.

Trey sat up and smiled at her. "As a matter of fact, my dear Iris, it does."

Iris motioned for him to keep going.

Trey turned his body toward her and clasped his hands together. "Here's the deal. My wonderful, but meddling, sister-in-law is deter-mined to see me happily involved with the one and only Macie Jo. A cute little pageant queen from the South. At present, I find myself averse to being involved with her. So I need your help. I want you to pretend to be my love interest for the foreseeable future, and in return, you can have as many rides as you'd like on that beautiful piece of machinery you see before you. I will even consider giving you lessons on how to ride it yourself, but that's negotiable." Sitting back, Trey flashed her a satisfied smile.

Iris eyed the motorcycle and then turned to look Trey up and down. She frowned, feeling tired all of a sudden.

"Look, gorgeous, I hate to turn down such a well-thought-out and tempting piece of bribery, but the answer's no. Sorry." She waved at Luke and Maggie, who had given up looking like they weren't spying on them from their front porch. They waved back guiltily and then turned and started talking to each other.

Trey frowned at Iris. "Fine, but you drive a hard bargain. Driving lessons. You can drive my bike yourself, *eventually*, but only if you're really convincing. I'm not letting you touch my keys if Sophie thinks you're faking."

Iris laughed and leaned back in her chair, wishing she had her leather jacket on. The air was starting to cool.

"Trey, how long has it been since a woman turned you down. For anything?" she asked, curious as to why he honestly thought he could convince her to do something there was no way she was going to do.

Trey's light blue eyes narrowed to slits and his arms looked bigger all of a sudden; he almost looked dangerous. Iris blinked.

"You really want to know? Try nine months ago. The woman I was in love with turned me down for Will Carson. And now the whole town of Alpine spends their spare time feeling bad for me. Trying to fix me. Throwing women at me left and right. Iris, let me explain something to you. Nothing is worse than a pity date. Hence, the need for you," he said, looking at her with a smidgeon of honest pleading in his eyes.

Iris's shoulders relaxed as she truly felt for him. "That would suck."

Trey's mouth edged up on one side, and he nodded his head in complete agreement.

"Fine, you're not the spoiled-rotten Ken doll I thought you were. We might actually have a little bit in common. I, um, just went through something similar myself. My ex had a problem with forsaking all others. Variety was the spice of his life. So I know what it's like to be gossiped about and pitied. I'm so sick of pity. I had to leave Seattle because I swear the pity was poisoning me. I felt like I would die from it," she said softly as she rubbed a speck of dust off her boot.

Trey frowned at the thread of agony he heard in Iris's voice and stayed silent.

"But I can't help you. Remember when we were talking in the store, and I might have mentioned how I hate men? Well, I wasn't kidding. It's not some junior high snit though. The thought of actually being near a man, or touching a man, or kissing a man kind of makes me physically ill. There's no way your little Sophie would buy you and me together, because right now . . . it makes me want to throw up. No offense."

Trey winced and kicked his own cowboy boots up by Iris's. His were brown, dusty, and well worn. "Well, that could be a problem. Do you mind if I still use just the idea of you? At least until I can find someone else. No fake dates, no smooching in front of my relatives. No nothing. I just want your permission to tell people that I'm madly in love with you. You don't have to do anything. You just have to be yourself and ignore the soap opera that is my life."

"Yuck." Iris shook her head, making her hair float around her face like a witch's bonfire.

Trey laughed and felt himself relax. "Yeah, I know. Yuck. I honestly can't think of anything worse than love right now. It tears your heart out, leaves you bleeding in a ditch, and makes your whole life gray and dead. But it would help me out and, let's be honest, you've fallen in love with my motorcycle."

Iris sighed at Trey's description. It was exactly how she felt, on both counts. "You're right about love *and* the motorcycle. It's sitting there calling my name. It's the most beautiful thing I've ever seen." Iris closed her eyes and knew that she was getting ready to make a huge mistake on more than one level. But she was on vacation. Mistakes are allowed when you're on vacation.

"Fine, I guess, but if I even think you're going in for a hug, or a kiss I swear my boots are going to find themselves embedded somewhere on your body."

Trey laughed and held his hand out to shake hers. "Deal."

Iris slipped her small, elegant hand into his and shook on it.

They were interrupted by Luke and Maggie walking up the porch steps. "Now isn't that a picture, Maggie?" Luke said.

Iris dropped her feet to the porch and sat up, wondering how much Luke might have heard. Trey was probably thinking the same thing, because he didn't look too happy either.

Maggie walked up the last step and stood next to her husband, looking worriedly back and forth between her and Trey. "Um, sure, Luke."

Luke grinned at both of them. "I was going to come over and talk to you about it tonight Iris, but it looks like Trey beat me to it."

Trey sat up and stared, confused, at Luke. "What are you talking about, Luke?"

Luke looked at Iris, his smile getting bigger and bigger. "Well, I just happened to mention to Sam this morning that my cousin Iris was in town and about how she's the most talented interior designer the Northwest has seen in ten years. Sam was crazy about the idea, Trey. He wants Iris to work with you on that new restaurant you're building. The other designer dropped out, so the timing is perfect. You guys will be working together. What do you think, Iris?"

Iris and Trey shared worried glances before she answered. "Well, I was kind of thinking about taking some time off before I regrouped and opened up shop here in Utah," she said, sounding strained.

Luke frowned and scratched his chin. "Iris, this is not a big deal,

34

seriously. It's nothing like the governor's mansion you won that award for. It's just a little restaurant. Think of it like a little side job so you don't get bored. Plus it will be a great way to introduce yourself to the people of Utah. They have no idea what a talented designer you are," he said loyally and with complete honesty.

Iris stood up and hugged her cousin properly. "Luke, you always were my favorite cousin. You are the kindest man. Tell you what. I'll go and talk to Sam tomorrow, and we'll see what needs to be done," she said, feeling a spark of interest in the project.

Luke laughed and gestured toward Trey. "Forget Sam. Trey's the project manager. Trey, meet your new designer."

Trey looked surprised and stood up to be on level with everyone else. "Well, I have to admit that I do find Iris's personal style very interesting. I can't wait to see what she can do with a whole building." He sounded more worried than intrigued.

Luke looked Iris up and down and blinked in surprise, just now noticing the changes in wardrobe and hair. "Uh, Iris, looks like you've, um . . . made some changes."

Maggie stepped forward and smiled encouragingly at Iris. "Well, I love the new look. The old you was beautiful and classy, don't get me wrong. But this new look, is just so powerful, isn't it?"

Iris grinned at Maggie. "Exactly! Really, who would want to mess with me when I'm wearing these boots, I ask you?"

Maggie nodded her head, her eyes filled with compassion. "I love them. As a matter of fact, I wish I had a pair. Except I'd want green ones."

Iris looked Maggie up and down and nodded. "That would look great on you. I don't think they come in green, though, but the man at the store told me he could have them special ordered."

Maggie smiled. "I'll order them tomorrow."

Iris decided to love Maggie right then, on the spot. Maggie grinned at her, deciding the same thing.

"Well, why don't I take you over and show you the restaurant? It's just a minute down the road. You can get a feel for the place," Trey offered.

Iris took in a deep breath and let it out slowly. "Life is just a little unexpected sometimes, isn't it?" she asked no one in particular, thinking of not only her new job but of Trey's proposition as well.

Maggie nodded her head in complete agreement.

Trey motioned for Iris to walk down first. "After you, Iris. And fortunately for me, I just happen to have an extra helmet," he said, smiling in satisfaction.

Iris waved at Maggie and Luke and walked slowly toward the black-and-silver Ducati, feeling slightly nervous now that she was so close to actually riding on one. Trey grabbed the extra helmet off the back and handed it to her. Black with streaks of flames on the side. Her mouth opened in awe as she took it in her hands and turned it slowly around.

"I love this," she whispered.

Trey laughed and took it out of her hands, slipping it on her head for her. "I had a feeling you would. Hop on, my little biker chick."

Iris waited for Trey to get on before she straddled the bike behind him. "But where do I put my hands?" she asked, her voice muffled by the helmet.

Trey turned around to look at her before he put his own helmet on. "Unfortunately, you're going to have to put your arms around me. Not in any weird way, just a nice, you-have-to-do-it-so-you-don't-die way."

Iris nodded. She could touch him. It creeped her out, but riding on his motorcycle was well worth it. He revved the engine, and seconds later she was zooming down the street, feeling the wind rush past her. She grinned and let out a whoop. She was probably squeezing the stuffing out of Trey, but she didn't care. It was scary. It was exhilarating. It was the most fun she'd had in way, way too long.

***

Luke and Maggie watched Iris and Trey disappear around the corner and then turned and looked at each other with very different expressions. Maggie looked very concerned, and Luke looked exultant.

"I'm calling my aunt Rachel tonight. Iris looks so happy. She's already interested in a great guy, and now she's going to work on a project. Life is back to normal. I knew Iris would be fine."

Maggie shook her head as they walked back toward their house. "I think you're jumping the gun, Luke. What were Trey and Iris shaking hands on when we walked up? And how did they even meet? They were supposed to meet through you. Something's up, but it's not romance. She doesn't look at him like a woman does when she's interested. She looks at him like he's a predator and she's trying to protect herself. She's put up as many defenses as she can. Her clothes, her hair, the boots. She's so vulnerable. Don't call your aunt yet. I think we're missing something."

Luke opened the front door to their house and ushered his wife inside. "The only thing I'm missing is dinner. Let's go grab Talon from your grandma and see if she made any extra."

Maggie grinned and shook her head. "What a mooch." But she grabbed the keys and raced him to the car. Just thinking of her grandma's cooking had her speeding down the road.

Chapter 8

Trey pulled his motorcycle into the parking lot next to the restaurant and waited for Iris to hop off. He took off his helmet and grabbed hers, laying them on the bike. Iris walked slowly toward the construction site, trying to take everything in. The location and the environment would have a big impact on the design, of course.

Trey gave her the tour, talking size and structure. The owners were retired chefs who had just moved from California. They'd always dreamed of starting their own restaurant, and now they were making it happen.

Iris walked through the tarp covering the front entrance while Trey made a call to the owners. They'd want to meet with her to go over their vision as soon as possible. She walked slowly through the space and felt herself smile. She'd come back tomorrow with her camera and take preliminary shots.

Trey pushed the tarp back and walked through, smiling as he approached her. "Rick and Sharon can meet with you Wednesday morning at ten. They can't wait. Sharon said she's heard of you before. They're both very excited to have you on the team," he said, sounding surprised.

Iris blushed and turned away. All of the attention she received from her work always made her uncomfortable. She just loved doing what she did best: making places beautiful.

"Perfect. That'll give me a day to come up with a few concepts to run by them. I'll come by tomorrow to do some sketches and take pictures.

It'll be fun," she said simply, still scanning the space as ideas came to her faster and faster.

Trey stood back and let Iris walk around for as long as she wanted to, but when his stomach started growling, he cleared his throat loudly.

"I hate to rush you, especially since you're being so nice to take on this project Luke and Sam just threw at you, but I'm starving to death."

Iris laughed and walked quickly toward him. "Sorry. If I start thinking, it's hard to stop. We can go now."

Trey held the tarp open for her, and they left as quickly as they came. He decided to take her on a short ride around Alpine just to give her a quick overview of her new home. Fifteen minutes later, though, they were back to her house.

Iris handed him the helmet and smiled gratefully. "If I could ride your motorcycle every day, I think I'd be the happiest person in the world."

Trey smiled at such a simple answer to happiness. "Well, then prepare to be incredibly happy, my dear Iris, because according to our deal, my motorcycle is at your beck and call as long as you're officially my fake girlfriend."

Iris grimaced at the word. "Sorry, but the thought of being somebody's girlfriend right now, even a fake one, is appalling. "

Trey nodded in agreement. "You'll get used to it. Well, I'm off to find some dinner. You're welcome to join me. I'll probably just grab a Subway or something."

Iris shook her head. "Nah, I've got an appointment to get a few tattoos."

Trey's eyebrows rose an inch, and he nodded his head silently. Iris grinned and turned away, waving her hand in the air. "See you tomorrow."

Trey watched her disappear into her house and wondered what she would show up with tomorrow. He got back on his bike and headed back to town. That was the nice thing about Iris. She wasn't boring.

Chapter 9

Iris woke up the next day feeling different. She lay in bed and tried to pinpoint it. Hopeful, maybe? Nah. It was more than hope. It was a new beginning. She *was* different. Her life was different. The future didn't seem so dark and depressing anymore.

She lifted her right arm and studied the henna patterns that ran every which way and grinned. Brittany had spent an hour drawing the lines and filling them in. The tattoos would only last a few weeks, but she would love every day she had them.

Tattoos, a new wardrobe, new hair, new job, and one beautiful motorcycle at her disposal. Iris gave up and giggled. Six days ago she would have never believed it. But right now, her heart was light and she was excited to start her new project.

Iris showered and then carefully chose one of her new outfits. She sighed in ecstasy at the real metal chain attached to her jeans. She picked a basic black T-shirt that would show off her tattoos perfectly. Sometimes understated was the better way to go. She slipped on her black boots and then focused on her makeup, going a little darker on the eyeliner than usual and picking a brand-new berry gloss. She stood back and studied the mirror, nodding her head. Definitely mean. She even looked a little scary today. Too bad she hadn't been wearing this outfit yesterday. Trey would have never had the gall to steal her ice cream. He'd have been way too intimidated.

She scowled at the mirror and then grinned. Perfect. She grabbed her sketchbook, camera, and the keys to her truck and ran out the door.

She arrived exactly two minutes later at the job site. After waving at a few framers and an electrician, Iris got to work, doing her best to ignore everyone. An hour had passed quickly when she heard a low, long whistle coming from behind her.

"Christmas has come early," a deep, gravely voice said behind her.

Iris lowered her pencil and turned her head to see a huge man, most likely Vin Diesel's twin brother, standing behind her grinning as if he had just won the Super Bowl. His black hair was spiky and went quite nicely with the large black gauge in his ear. His nose looked like it had been smashed in a few times, but overall he looked like a nice man. He must be excited to have a designer on the job.

"Hi," Iris said in a polite, friendly way and then went back to work.

"Honey, I don't know where you came from, or why you're here, but I need to send someone a thank-you card, because I have just fallen in love."

Iris frowned, turning back around to face the imposing man. He really was huge, and his arms were covered in real tattoos, not the fake henna ones she had. Yep, one of them looked like Satan. And he was looking at her like she was Sunday dinner and he hadn't eaten in months. Time to shut this guy down.

"I'm Iris Levine. I'll be working on this project with Trey Kellen. I'm just doing some preliminary sketches before I meet with the owners tomorrow. Let me know if I'm in your way," she said dismissively.

The man's eyebrows went up. "You're the designer Trey was telling me about this morning? Wow. I would have never guessed. I never imagined a serious designer could look like you. You're the most beautiful thing I've ever seen in my life," the man said with such blatant honesty that Iris had to smile.

She heard boots hitting gravel and turned to see Trey running fast toward them.

"Donny, I see you've met Iris," Trey said, looking back and forth worriedly between the two of them.

Iris opened her mouth to say something, but Donny rushed in. "Trey, why in the world didn't you warn me about Iris. I about had a heart attack standing here trying to take it all in."

Iris blushed and started to feel a little uncomfortable. What had happened to her invisible Stay-the-Heck-Away-from-Me sign she'd posted on her forehead? The tattoos, the chains, the black, the hair?

Trey nodded his head and patted Donny on the shoulder. "Now why would I want to do that? I don't want you trying to steal my girlfriend."

Donny made a huffing noise and shook his head, continuing to stare at Iris. "She's not your type, Trey. She's mine. Look at her. She's perfect. No way is she your girlfriend."

Iris started feeling panicky and looked at Trey, silently pleading for help. Trey winked at her, his light blue eyes practically sparkling at the position she was in.

"Sorry, Donny, but I found her first," he said and then stepped around Donny to gently and slowly put his arm around Iris's shoulders, completely breaking one of her rules.

Iris bit her lip but didn't say anything, so Trey cleared his throat and faced the doubting giant in front of him.

"But regardless of my passionate regard for Iris, she has been hired by Sam to design the restaurant, so we both need to be careful not to let our feelings get in the way of work. I'd hate for Iris to feel uncomfortable being on the jobsite," he said, his voice sounding firm and with an unmistakable warning.

Donny nodded his head as his shoulders fell. "Gotcha, boss. It was nice meeting you, Iris," he said looking at her soulfully one last time.

Iris and Trey watched as Donny went back inside the building. When she could no longer see Donny's massive shoulders, she let a shaky breath out. She stepped away from Trey, forcing his arm to drop and turned to face him.

"Oh. My. Heck."

Trey laughed softly and reached out to grab a strand of fiery red hair. "What? You're surprised?"

Iris shoved her hands in her pockets and kicked a rock. "Well, yeah! I've done everything but put a sign on my back that says stay back. Maybe he's dyslexic."

Trey laughed again and reached out taking her arm in his hands as he studied the tribal tattoos in dark brown that ran from her wrist to her shoulder.

"Well, there's one thing you forgot. Men. You're obviously used to a certain type of man. You're back off sign that works so well for the successful, business-suit-wearing, corporate kind of guy actually does the opposite for my dear friend Donny. You see, there's a whole population of men who will take one look at you and start to believe in heaven again."

Iris's mouth fell open in horror at her giant mistake. "Oh, no."

Trey laughed at her expression and gently lowered her arm. "Oh, yes. But you don't need to worry. Because as much as your being my fake girlfriend will protect me from beautiful pageant queens, I am here to protect you from one of the best plumbers I've ever known. Super nice guy, by the way. I'm almost certain he owns an actual Harley."

Iris swallowed nervously and turned her head, watching all the construction workers walk around them, doing their jobs. But she'd have to be blind not to realize that some of them were openly checking her out.

Trey grabbed her chin and forced her to look at him. "Just ignore it. I'll pass it around that you and I are together and no one will bother you. I promise. And if someone crosses the line, I'll deal with him."

Iris stared up into Trey's serious blue eyes and felt herself relax. She trusted him. "Okay."

Trey smiled almost gently at her and ignored her feelings about being hugged and hugged her tightly. Iris immediately stiffened but relaxed as he patted her back comfortingly.

"Face it. We need each other." He let her go, walking toward the building and grabbing his phone at the same time.

Iris ran forward before he could disappear. "Hey! When do I get my ride on your motorcycle today?"

Trey looked back over his shoulder and shrugged. "I'll come by your house after four sometime. I'll take you for a ride around the Alpine Loop. You'll love it."

Iris watched him disappear and smiled. She was a full-blown motorcycle junkie now. She grabbed her camera out of her pocket and began taking pictures. She finished up a half-hour later and only had one more awkward moment when she came face-to-face with Donny on her way to her truck. He was carrying a bunch of takeout boxes from Iceberg and stumbled since he was staring at her and didn't see a sledgehammer someone had left lying around. The boxes flew out of his hands. It would have been rude if she hadn't helped him pick them up. Trey showed up seconds later, though, pushing her toward her truck and scolding Donny for being a klutz.

Iris smiled to herself and jumped in her truck. It was a comforting feeling knowing that Trey would make sure all of the men gave her space while at the same time not making any moves on her himself. Iris rolled down the window and let the wind whip through her flaming hair as she drove home. She had a lot of work to do before her meeting with the owners. And when it came to her work, she was a professional.

Chapter 10

Maggie, Sophie, Jacie, and Allison sat around a table at Costa Vida talking and, for the most part, smiling. It was their monthly ritual to meet for lunch at their favorite Mexican restaurant. Sophie was the only one not joining in the conversation.

"Margaret Petersen. What have you done?" Sophie finally asked, piercing Maggie with accusing eyes.

Allison and Jacie turned wide eyes on their friend and forgot all about their food. Maggie looked down at her salad and smiled brightly. "Well, I think the mango chicken salad is amazing. I'll give you a bite if you want," she said, holding her fork out to Sophie.

Sophie sneered at the fork and pointed to her salad. "Sweet pork beats out mango chicken any day of the week, and you know what I'm talking about. Your cousin Iris is a psycho, and she already has her claws in Trey!"

Maggie stopped smiling and put her fork down, staring Sophie down. Jacie and Allison exchanged worried looks. Maggie was easygoing unless she was mad. If she was mad, no one with half a brain would get in her way.

"Excuse me? Did you just call Iris a psycho?" Maggie asked in a deadly serious voice, her eyes turning stormy.

Sophie held up her hand but didn't back down. "Don't get offended. But when we started this whole stupid thing, we swore that Trey's welfare was our number-one priority. We all agreed. And your cousin looks

45

like a truck stop waitress from some reality TV show. She has tattoos!" Sophie yelled across the table.

Maggie leaned forward in her chair. "They're henna! I'm getting some myself next week. And don't you dare call her some truck stop waitress. She's a college graduate and one of the best designers in the Northwest She's famous in Seattle. Don't you put her down. You have no idea what she's been through."

Sophie crossed her arms and dug in. "Well, I do dare. And I don't care what she did in Seattle, because she's in Alpine now, and Trey says he's dating her. She is completely wrong for him. *Completely*. Have you seen her hair!" She proceeded to throw her napkin on the table, turning red in the face.

Maggie nodded, looking dangerous. "As a matter of fact, I have. And I love it. I don't see one thing wrong with her hair. And if you're using Iris's hair as a reason for her not being good enough for Trey, then I think that's pretty shallow."

Sophie gasped. "Did you just call me shallow?"

Maggie stared at her unblinking. "You've just trashed my cousin because of her clothes and her hair without asking anything about who she really is. So, yes, I think I am."

Sophie stood up and looked at Jacie and Allison, who were staring at her in open-mouthed shock. "I'm not going to stay here and listen to this anymore. I'm very disappointed in you, Maggie," she said as she grabbed her purse off the back of her chair and started to walk away.

"Get used to disappointment, Sophie. I've got a news flash for you. This world is about more than hair and makeup." Maggie called out, looking furious.

Jacie and Allison watched as Sophie banged out of Costa Vida and then turned and stared at Maggie.

"What just happened?" Jacie demanded.

Allison pushed a water cup toward Maggie. "Maggie, what's going on?"

Maggie unclenched her teeth and took a sip of her water obediently. Her blues eyes looked like ice chips and her hands were balled up on the table. Jacie, who was famous for being pretty feisty herself, was in awe.

"I love Iris. I think she's amazing. She's beautiful, she's resilient, and she's a fighter. Trey Kellen would be the luckiest man in the world to have Iris," she stated looking madder and madder.

Allison shared a look of concern with Jacie as they both scooted their chairs closer to Maggie. Allison rubbed her back soothingly. "Sweetie, just relax. Sophie's gone. It's just me and Jacie here. Now, tell us what's going on."

Maggie sighed and rubbed her temples. She took a bite of her mango salad before pushing it away and grabbing Sophie's forgotten sweet pork salad.

"Well, she's right about one thing. The sweet pork is better than the mango chicken. But she's wrong about Iris. Iris is probably the perfect woman for Trey. She's a match for him physically, intellectually, and personality-wise. But Iris just happens to be going through a hard time right now. She feels used and broken, and she's trying to get her power back. Granted, she's trying to do that in creative ways, but she's trying. She's not lying down and dying just because the man she was in love with broke her heart."

Allison and Jacie shared a commiserating glance.

"I don't even like Macie Jo," Jacie said, taking a bite of her smothered burrito. "Trey would hate her after five minutes, guaranteed."

Allison nodded her head. "I checked out Macie Jo yesterday. I went in to get my nails done, and I wasn't impressed. She spent the entire time talking about her days on the pageant circuit. I mean, she's nice and everything, but I'm willing to give Iris a chance. Tell us what happened with the man she was in love with."

Maggie winced and quietly explained. "His name is Riley Shelton, and she spent two years planning the perfect wedding. She found out on her wedding day that he had been cheating on her with two other women for sure, but possibly more. One of his girlfriends showed up at the reception and showed her all the proof. Texts, pictures, emails, everything. There was no doubt. Iris confronted Riley and then walked up to the stage and announced that the wedding was over. She told everyone thank you for coming and to please take their present home with them. She apologized for canceling the party and then walked off the stage with more dignity than I could have. She's amazing. And I was there. I saw her do it."

Allison shook her head and groaned in sympathy. "Men."

Jacie nodded in agreement. "Poor thing. So, um . . . is she still married to this guy?"

Maggie shook her head vehemently. "Her dad sicced a lawyer on the situation that same day. She got an annulment. At least I think she did."

Jacie sighed in relief. "Well, at least she didn't find out after the honeymoon."

Allison winced, looking ill. "It could always be worse."

"So what's the deal with the hair and tattoos? Why's Sophie so bent out of shape?" Jacie demanded.

Maggie smiled and shook her head. "Well, as you can imagine, Iris wants to take a little break. She moved here to get away from Riley and that whole situation, but she's taking a break from her old self too. She's trying out new things. Not in a bad way. It's all innocent. You should see these boots she's been wearing. I've never seen a woman get such a kick out of footwear. I had to order some myself. They're coming in next week. But yeah, her hair is interesting."

Allison smiled and took a bite of her nachos. "Sophie does take hair very seriously. But what could be so bad that Sophie would get so angry?"

Maggie grabbed a notebook out of her purse and started sketching in quick, sure lines. She explained, "It's kind of like this. Remember the painting I showed you at the gallery? Well, it's jagged now and she had the tips dyed a fiery red. If she were a rock star, it'd be perfect. It's a little much for Alpine, but she's enjoying herself. And I swear, if anyone gives her a hard time about her stinking boots or her hair, they'll have me to deal with."

Jacie grimaced and picked up the paper. "Ah, yes. Macie Jo was talking about doing a customer's hair like this. She loved it. Iris gave Macie Jo a fifty-dollar tip. Wow."

Allison tilted her head and studied the sketch. "You know, her hair was so long to begin with, if she trims off the jagged tips, she'd look exactly like she did before. It's not like she shaved her head or anything. She'll get tired of it eventually."

Maggie smiled. "The flames are growing on me."

Jacie took a sip of her drink. "So now what? This situation has gotten a little out of control. Sophie is madder than I've seen her in a long time, and Maggie, honey, *I* wouldn't even mess with you. But we're all friends, and we really do want to help Trey. So where do we go from here?"

Allison looked pained. She hated confrontation. Jacie looked torn.

She was Sophie's best friend, but she was with Maggie on this one. And Maggie had dug in her heels. She was a protective person by nature, and Iris had brought out her instincts by the busload. No way was she going to let Sophie make her feel like less than she was.

Maggie took a huge bite of Sophie's pork salad and shrugged. "It's called an apology. Sophie's going to have to figure out how to make one."

Jacie looked out the window of the restaurant and sighed. Like that was ever going to happen.

Allison reached over and tried a bite of Sophie's salad too. "She'll come around."

Maggie shrugged. "If Iris wants Trey, then she gets him. Sophie better not get in her way."

Maggie enjoyed eating the rest of Sophie's salad as Jacie and Allison changed the subject and talked about the new restaurant. The real question was, did Iris even want Trey?

Chapter 11

Iris rolled her shoulders to loosen up her cramped muscles and glanced at the clock. All of her sketches were finished, and she'd written out her notes for her meeting with Rick and Sharon tomorrow morning. It was only two in the afternoon, so she had time before Trey showed up. She wandered outside to check the mail. Breathing in the fresh air, she glanced around. It really was a charming, old-fashioned neighborhood and completely opposite of her condo back in Seattle. She thought of it, perfectly decorated and sitting empty. She'd have to call her mom and dad later to ask them to lease it out. She had a feeling she was going to be staying in Alpine for a while.

Smiling, Iris pulled the mail from her mailbox and noticed an official-looking manila envelope. Her stomach dropped and her smile vanished as she read the name of her lawyer on the return address. She hurried back into the house.

Opening the envelope, Iris pulled out the official annulment documents, signed and sealed by the judge. It was done. Her four-hour marriage didn't exist anymore. She let the papers slip from her fingers and stared out the window. All of the feelings she had bottled up and ignored for so long rushed out. Tears wet her cheeks. Ignoring the papers on the floor, she walked upstairs to the spare bedroom where a box sat, still sealed with tape. Going to the box, she ripped off the tape. She pulled out the photo album on top and sat cross-legged on the floor.

Opening the album, she saw a picture of Riley holding her skis for her on one of their many skiing trips. She studied the picture critically.

He looked so happy. She looked so happy. But from all the emails she'd received from Cherish, even then he had been cheating on her. It was all a big lie.

She went through the pictures in the two photo albums that made up her life with Riley Shelton, seeing them for what they were. A sad, horrible mistake. Then she picked up both albums and walked down the stairs and out of the house to the garbage can. She opened the lid and dumped the pictures in. It was time to throw the garbage out.

Wiping her hands on her jeans, she sighed. *Now what?* She stared up at the cloud-covered sky and decided she needed a treat. Something new. Something wonderful that she'd always wanted. Ice cream and hot pockets weren't going to do it this time. It had to be bigger. It had to be fun. It had to be perfect.

She leaned up against her truck, thinking. As she realized exactly what she needed, she gasped. Running into the house, she grabbed her keys and purse and ran even faster back to her truck. She paused with her hand on the steering wheel, laughing at herself. She had no idea where to go. Using her phone to look up an address, she then calmly pulled out into the street. She'd waited her whole life for this; she didn't need to rush it.

An hour later, she returned with Sally, her new cock-a-poo. Half cocker spaniel and half poodle. Sally had caramel-colored curls and the cutest personality. She was six years old and spoiled rotten. The previous owners had gotten too old to take care of her and had to take her to the shelter. They hadn't been able to take her on too many walks either, so Sally had a weight problem. Iris adored her. After taking Sally on a walk around the neighborhood, Iris sat on the front porch with her dog, feeding her treats and trying to teach her how to shake hands. It wasn't working. She got down on the porch next to Sally, put her arms around the dog, and leaned her head on the dog's soft fur.

"It's okay, Sally. I'll love you anyway."

"That rule about hugging really was a pain, wasn't it?" Trey said, walking up the concrete sidewalk. He smiled at the picture of the tough-looking woman hugging a dog.

Iris smiled and sat up, letting go of Sally. Sally went into guard-dog mode and growled at Trey, blocking him from the porch. She actually sounded kind of menacing too.

Trey just laughed and held out his hand for Sally to sniff. "Throw me one of those dog treats. Looks like I need to make friends with your pit bull."

Iris threw the little bag of treats to Trey. Sally fixed her eyes on Trey, her stubby tail beating wildly. She was a complete sucker for a good-looking face. Iris would have to have a serious talk with her later.

"Trey, meet Sally. Sally, meet the man in my life, Trey Kellen."

Trey grinned and raised his eyebrow at her as he held the treat above Sally's head. "Sit. Sit. Sit," he commanded. When Sally finally obeyed, he gave her the treat, petting her and telling her what a good girl she was.

"Sally, you are one pretty little dog."

Iris managed a smile as she watched Trey played with her dog. He glanced at her now and then and finally joined her on the porch.

"How are you, beautiful?" Trey asked gently, taking her hand in his.

Iris stared at his large masculine hand holding hers and decided not to make an issue of it. Besides, it felt kind of nice. "Oh, just one of those days, I guess," she answered quietly, looking away.

Trey nodded and then reached down to pet Sally with his other hand. "We're in this together, Iris. I've told you things about me that I don't discuss with anyone. Tell me what's wrong."

Iris's face crumpled and she leaned forward, resting her forehead on her free hand.

"It's nothing, really." Trey sat in silence, waiting for her to continue. "I just got my annulment papers in the mail today. It's official. My marriage never happened. *Oh, how I wish it had never happened.* Why wasn't I smarter? Why was I so stupid? I couldn't even see that the man I loved was cheating on me?" Her voice wavered with unshed tears.

Trey let go of her hand and reached over, picking her up and placing her on his lap as if she weighed nothing. He then wrapped his arms around her and let her rest her head on his shoulder.

"It hurts, doesn't it?"

Iris nodded, feeling a little better.

"Tell me what happened," he said softly.

Iris groaned and shook her head, but found herself telling Trey everything. Trey rubbed her back soothingly as she poured her heart out. All the betrayal, the shock, the pain, and the incredible humiliation she still felt every time she remembered flooded through her with more force than ever.

"Sweetie, it's his shame. Not yours," Trey said firmly, pushing her hair out of her eyes.

"That's how it should be, huh? But it's not. It's my shame. He shamed me. And then when the truth was out, instead of feeling sorry, he and his family trashed me to all their friends and most of mine. It was like he had to tear me down to justify his actions. In the end, it turned out *he* was the victim. There had to be something wrong with me for him to do all the things he did. And his family agreed. His sister, his mother, his aunts. All of these people who treated me like I was a part of their family and thought I was the best thing that ever happened to Riley, now told everyone they could find how controlling and demanding I was. How I made Riley so miserable that he had no choice but to find happiness with other women. He turned it completely around and made everything my fault. And the worst part was his anger. He was enraged that I had the nerve to call off the marriage. He was furious that I didn't just keep my mouth shut and pretend like everything was fine."

As Iris finished, she waited for Trey to say something. *Anything.* Instead, his arms tightened around her. She finally looked up into his face and noticed that his jaw looked like granite. He looked down and rubbed her arm. "Riley is a joke. Worse than that, he's weak. Blaming his faults on a sweet woman like you is ridiculous, but sadly, not new. Men have been doing that since the beginning of time. I'm sorry it happened to you. I truly am," he said honestly, looking deep into her eyes, and wiping her last tear away.

Iris sniffed and then gave him a watery smile. "You know, it's really too bad you stole my ice cream," she said as she gingerly got off his lap and stood looking shy and slightly embarrassed.

Trey smiled and stood up next to her. "And why's that?"

"I might have had to give up my ban on men. But lucky for you, the ban is still firmly in place," she said with a grin.

"Yeah, lucky for me," Trey said, without smiling.

Iris put Sally in the backyard and then met Trey by his motorcycle. He took her for a ride around the Alpine Loop, stopping to show her the different mountains, explaining their names and the history of the region. Iris loved every second and felt regret when they drove up to her house.

"Trey, that was amazing. And I haven't done anything yet to earn my motorcycle privileges. If you want me to meet Sophie and talk to her, I'll tell her how amazing I think you are. I won't even be lying," she said with a smile.

Trey smiled gently at her as he reached for her helmet. "I'll give you a little more time before I throw you to the wolves."

Iris laughed and flexed her arms. "I am so much tougher than I look. I can handle Sophie," she promised.

Trey smiled and shocked them both by leaning in and giving her a quick kiss on the cheek. "You let me handle Sophie for now. You just get used to being my girlfriend first."

Iris blushed, not sure if he was kidding. She waved as he disappeared around the corner and made her way back to her house.

"Iris! Hold up."

Iris turned to see Maggie walking toward her with a beautiful little boy in her arms. "Hey there, Maggie. How's it going?"

Maggie smiled and pushed a silken lock of her son's hair off his forehead. "I'm great. By the way, this is Talon. You met him at that family reunion a year and a half ago, but he was just a baby then."

Iris smiled at the serious little boy with light brown hair and bright blue eyes. "Hi, Talon. Would you like to meet my new dog, Sally?" she asked him, hoping he'd say yes.

Maggie grinned. "Really? You got a dog? I never pictured you as a dog person."

Iris laughed and led them to the back of her house, opening the gate for them to walk through. "You're right, I wasn't. Too busy, for one thing. And Riley hated dogs. But it turns out, that I am a dog person. Meet Sally, the new love of my life," she said as her cock-a-poo came bounding around the corner, barking happily. She jumped up on Iris's knees, her tongue hanging out.

"Oh she's beautiful, Iris," Maggie said, bending down to pet the dog. Sally immediately turned her tummy up for a scratch. "Wow, she's not shy, is she?" Maggie said laughing.

Talon was nervous around Sally at first, but then he giggled and ventured a hand out to touch the soft curls.

As Iris saw the glow on Maggie's face as she watched her child giggle in delight, her heart felt better. "I wish I could paint this moment right now," Iris said softly.

Maggie grinned. "That's funny, the lady that used to live here a couple years ago was obsessed with dogs and had your house covered in paintings of them. They weren't good paintings either. Imagine dogs playing cards, sitting at a table," she said with a laugh.

Iris shook her head. "No, I meant you with your son. Your expression just now was one of the most beautiful things I've ever seen. It was love at its purest."

Maggie tilted her head and smiled at Iris. "I like that. You know, I'm so busy painting everybody else that I haven't had a portrait done of us. I've had photos taken, but I'd love one of me and my son," she said wistfully.

Iris looked bashful for a second but stuck her hands in her pockets and smiled shyly. "I paint. It's a hobby of mine. I'm not as good as you are, of course, but if you're willing, I'd love to paint you and Talon. I don't have too much going on, and it'd be fun for me."

Maggie looked surprised. "I had no idea! I knew you were artistic because you're so good with color and textures. That's why you're so good at your job. But I didn't know that you paint. Yeah. I'd love a portrait. You can borrow my paints and brushes. Just say when."

Iris laughed and studied the little boy and her dog. "Well, I do things a little differently. I take a bunch of pictures and go from there. I don't do well with live sittings. It's too much pressure. But maybe tomorrow sometime. I can take a few shots, or if you have a favorite picture you already have, I can work from that."

Maggie thought about it for a second. "I might already have one. Let me go through my pictures, and I'll see what I can find."

The two women talked for a few more minutes before Maggie picked up Talon. "I better go get started on dinner. Luke always comes home ravenous. Banking is so draining," she said with a laugh.

Iris followed Maggie into the front yard, shutting the gate firmly and promising Sally that she'd come back soon.

"I believe it. Listen, Maggie, if you ever want to go to lunch or for a walk, let me know. I'd love to hang out." She offered, holding her hand up to shade her eyes from the setting sun.

Maggie smiled, her eyes lighting up. "I was just getting ready to say the same exact thing! I'll see you tomorrow when I find the picture, and we'll plan something. I have a couple other friends I'd like you to meet too. Really amazing women," she promised.

Iris rubbed her arms against the cool weather and nodded her head.

"I would love it. Thanks, Maggie. Bye, Talon," she said with a wave and headed into her little house.

Turning on the porch light, Iris began to shut the blinds. She watched with a sad smile as Luke pulled into the driveway and jumped out of his car, he picked up his wife and son, swinging them around. She could barely hear their laughter. Leaning her head against the window, she felt a painful yearning. What would it be like to have a beautiful child to love? And a husband who loved her, *only* her? From what she could tell on Maggie's face, it was pretty amazing.

Chapter 12

Trey kept his eye on Big Donny when the clock hit ten thirty. He didn't want Donny making a beeline for Iris when she showed up. He was trying to get her comfortable with men, and Donny wasn't helping. Rick and Sharon were already there, walking around the job site, holding hands, and talking menus. Rick was a short man, large in the middle, bald as a cue ball, and an expert at steak. Sharon was his perfect mate. Short, plump, and full of energy. Trey had no idea what color her hair was because she wore a different colored bandana every time he saw her. They were good people, and Trey wanted to see them get their dream. He hoped there was more to Iris than just hype. As it was, she was late. He glanced at his watch and noticed the time was now ten thirty-one. *Unprofessional, Iris,* he thought with a shake of his head.

Trey headed over to Rick and Sharon to distract them and noticed someone was ahead of him. He noticed the legs first. Long, lean, and ending in three-inch, killer black heels. The black pencil skirt went well with the legs and heels. And the cream silk shirt tucked in at a tiny waist had him wondering who this woman was. Why was she here talking to the owners? Insurance? A lawyer? He walked faster, unable to keep his eyes off the elegant neck and upswept hair. Her hair was dark but glowed with a quiet fire. The woman turned her head as he joined the circle and smiled brightly.

"Hey, Trey. I was wondering where you were. I want you in on our meeting. Rick, Sharon, let me show you some drawings I made, and then I want you to tell me what you think."

Trey's mouth fell open. All the way. The gorgeous businesswoman in front of him screamed class, money, and success. She opened a black leather portfolio and gestured for the owners to follow her inside. Trey followed at a distance, knowing he had absolutely nothing to contribute. Iris Levine was a stone-cold killer. There was no flame-tipped hair, no ripped jeans, or even her black boots. He barely recognized her.

"What happened to Iris?" Donny whispered in his ear, pulling Trey back into himself.

Trey shook his head in wonder. "I think, Donny, that it's possible we're seeing the real Iris."

Donny shook his head, looking disappointed. "I liked her better yesterday," he said and walked off with fifty pounds of pipe on his shoulder.

Trey looked Iris up and down again and asked himself which Iris he preferred. If this had been the woman he met in the grocery store, would he have stolen her ice cream? Probably not. This Iris was intimidating. Far more so than the biker chick she was yesterday.

Trey obediently followed Iris around, smiling proudly at her competence and the confident way she spoke and gestured with her hands. She was in her element. She was taking Rick and Sharon's vision and helping them see it in a new light. And from Rick and Sharon's delighted awe, she was doing a good job of it.

When they were done, Trey walked Rick and Sharon to their car. He promised to call them tomorrow and then shut their door, walking back toward Iris.

She pushed a stray piece of hair that had fallen out of its twist behind her ear and glanced up when she heard his boots on the gravel. "They really like modern, Trey. It'll go great with their menu. I'm so excited. I did one restaurant in Seattle last year in an ultra-modern style. Have you seen the concrete sculptures Zach Mason does? I'm going to call him and see if he's busy. One of his pieces would make an amazing statement if we put it right in the middle and then placed the tables almost in a circle around it. I'm seeing a small tasteful water feature and a few romantic small tables for two in the center areas."

Trey grinned as he listened to her, liking the way she used her hands and sketched for him as easily as most people breathed. He liked Iris. As she talked, the same stray lock of hair fell forward. He pushed it behind her ear as she finished her latest sketch.

"We are so lucky to have you," he said softly, watching her face glow with excitement. Her bright green eyes lit up her face.

Iris looked up and paused as she saw the goofy look on his face. "What? Oh, I'm happy to do this. I needed a little project, and this is perfect."

Iris shoved her sketches into her portfolio and sighed happily. She slipped the strap over her shoulder and then looked past him. Trey watched as the color drained from her face and her bright-green eyes turned bleak and forlorn. Looking over his shoulder in alarm, expecting Big Donny, Trey was surprised to see a man his own age in a dark blue suit walking toward them. He had wavy, light brown, artistically styled hair and a careless smile. But it was his swagger that automatically set Trey's teeth on edge. He knew guys like this.

The man took one look at Trey, in his jeans, flannel shirt, and dusty boots, and then zeroed in on Iris.

"Darling. I've been searching everywhere for you. What in the world are you doing here?" he asked, looking around himself with an obvious sneer in his voice.

Iris tore her eyes away from the man walking toward them and looked at Trey with agony in her eyes, as if she were asking for help. This had to be Riley. Trey stepped in closer to Iris. She didn't have her new armor on, but she had him.

"Iris, you didn't tell me your accountant was coming today," Trey said, pulling Iris to his side, his arm snug around her waist. "Reschedule, sweetie. We've got plans." Trey said this last sentence with just enough warmth in his voice to make Riley wonder what those plans were.

Iris didn't say anything. She was frozen. Riley came to stand a few feet away from them, taking in the fact that Trey's arm was around his ex-wife. He looked stunned. Trey smiled and leaned over to kiss the top of Iris's head.

"Iris, love, introduce me to your friend here," he ordered, nudging Iris with his hip. She needed to stand up to Riley now or she'd regret it.

Iris cleared her throat and looked Riley straight in the eye. "Trey, I'd like you to meet my ex-husband, Riley Shelton. Riley, meet Trey Kellen, my boyfriend," she said with just a slight waver to her voice.

Trey took it from there. "Ah. Riley. The one and only. Riley, I have to shake your hand. If it weren't for you being the dumbest man in the world, I wouldn't have the love of my life." Trey grabbed Riley's hand and shook it so firmly that it was just shy of physical assault. Riley winced noticeably and flexed his fingers as soon Trey let go.

Trey put his arm back around Iris, mostly to keep her standing up straight. He wasn't completely sure she wasn't getting wobbly around the knees.

"Touch me again, and I'll have you behind bars," Riley warned Trey, his cold light eyes furious. He turned back to Iris. "We need to talk, darling. I've made a lot of mistakes. I know that now. But I'm begging for the chance to make it up to you. When you left, I felt like dying. I acted badly. I acted like a jerk. I'm disgusted with myself. Let's go somewhere where we can talk. I'm going to do whatever I have to, to get you back. I'm prepared to do anything."

Trey felt Iris start to shake and was about to open his mouth to tell the jerk to get off the lot when Iris finally spoke.

"You couldn't do anything, you couldn't say anything, to get me back Riley. We're done. We were done the minute I found out about all of your women. Just leave," she said quietly but firmly.

Trey felt his chest puff out with pride. She was holding her own.

Riley smiled charmingly and reached out to touch Iris's arm. Trey snarled and Riley quickly dropped his arm. "Iris, get rid of your guard dog. Did you really think I'd buy for a second that you'd be interested in this man. What, is he some hired hand that you've ordered to scare me off? Your taste in everything, from clothes to architecture to men, is the finest. This man looks like a mutt if I've ever seen one. Now stop being obstinate and let's have a serious conversation like adults. No more running from confrontation, Iris. I have my faults, but so do you. I think it's high time that you take responsibility for your part in our break up. A relationship is a two-way street. And I was honestly hurting inside. Do you really think I would have turned to those women if I felt the love I needed to feel from you?"

Trey glanced down at Iris's stricken face and felt anger course through his blood. But if he let go of her to punch Riley in the face, she would end up in the dirt. He saw Big Donny walking by and grinned evilly.

"Donny! This man is being a nuisance to Iris. He sounds like a crazed stalker to me. Will you please remove him from the premises? You know how much I hate it when Iris is upset," he ordered, his voice sounding deadly.

He shouldn't have enjoyed the look of horror on Riley's face as Donny's eyes turned mean and hard. But he did. Donny could move quite fast for a man that weighed close to two fifty. Riley squeaked like a third-grader when Donny grabbed his arm and forced him to his tip-toes, quickly escorting him back to his car. Trey grinned with relish as he saw Donny's mouth move and Riley's face turning paler and paler. Donny had just earned himself a big bonus.

"Iris, are you okay?" Trey said, moving to block her from the sight of Riley being shoved into his rental car.

Iris blinked a few times and swallowed. "Of course. Thank you, Trey. I'm fine. Really," she said trying to peek over his shoulder.

Trey turned to see if Riley was on his way. But he wasn't. He was sitting in his car in the lot next to the building site, staring at Iris. Trey's mouth hardened, and he turned back to Iris. "Iris, come on."

Iris swallowed and clenched her hands nervously. "I am so sorry for what I'm about to do. I know you're a woman-free zone, so I promise to make this up to you, but I just have to do it."

Trey looked down at her in confusion. She whispered sorry one more time, then gripped his face in her cold hands and bent his head down to hers. She kissed him as if her life depended on it. Trey's eyes widened in shock. It took him a second to grasp the situation, but when he did, he wrapped his arms around Iris's waist, lifting her off the ground and tilting his head to kiss her back. His mom always bragged that he was a fast learner. At least two minutes later, Trey lifted his head, dazed and breathing faster than he had when he ran the Alpine 5k last month.

Iris opened her green eyes that were now brighter than he'd ever seen them and grinned at him. "I am so sorry," she said. She didn't sound sorry at all. Laughing softly, she wiped some lipstick off his mouth.

Trey lowered Iris to the ground and reached around, taking the clasp out of her hair. He smiled contentedly as her hair fell in a flame-tipped curtain. "Are you trying to kill me, Iris?"

Iris blushed and shook her head. "I don't think a kiss from me will kill anyone off."

Trey grinned as he saw Riley's car drive quickly out of the lot and down the street. "Oh, I disagree. My heart is beating so fast I might need some mouth-to-mouth resuscitation."

Iris laughed and punched his arm. "You're hilarious. But seriously.

Thank you. That was going above and beyond. I disregarded your woman-free zone, and you were a very good sport about it."

Trey grinned at her and grabbed her hand. "I'll try to forgive you. What I don't think I'll get over is the fact that he had the nerve to call me a mutt. I've never been so hurt in all my life. Is he right, Iris? Am I not good enough for you?" he asked trying to look hurt.

Iris's eyes turned a cold green and her hands bunched into fists. "*Oooh,* I hate when he does that. He's so good at making people feel like they're not good enough. Trey, of course you are. And if I wasn't on a break from men, and you weren't on a break from women, I promise I'd rather be with you over Riley any day. You're so much nicer than him. You're the sweetest, most genuine man in the world. Honestly, if you weren't an ice cream thief, I'd think you were perfect," she said kindly, patting him on the cheek.

Trey grabbed her hand and held it over his heart. "Now, as I recall, you actually got a free carton of Chunky Monkey delivered right to your house. I think forgiveness is long, long overdue."

Iris pulled her hand away and laughed. "Fine. You're forgiven. Oh, Trey, I didn't even have my boots on," she said, sounding sincerely heartbroken.

He slung his arm across her shoulders and walked with her toward the truck. "Sweetheart, for you, I will hunt him down and bring him back here, so you can practice kicking him with your lethal boots."

Iris grinned at the thought. "Really? Because I can run home and be back in about fifteen minutes."

Trey shook his head and laughed. "You are one crazy woman, you know that?"

Iris smiled proudly and nodded her head. "I didn't think so before, but I'm determined to be one now."

Trey frowned as a red convertible drove into the parking lot and stopped right beside them. Macie Jo slid out of the car and walked toward them, smiling so brightly he didn't even need to wonder what was going on.

"Hi, Macie!" Iris said. "Look at my hair. The red has only faded a little bit. But I like it this way. What do you think?"

Macie stopped grinning at Trey as she finally noticed Iris standing beside him. "Oh, Iris, I didn't see you standing there. My, your hair does look good. You must have had the best stylist in town," she said with a dimple showing in her cheek.

"What are you doing here?" Iris asked curiously.

Trey grimaced, knowing exactly what she was doing here. Why couldn't Sophie just let it go?

"Oh, my boss wanted me to bring Trey here a little lunch. We had an open house today at the salon to introduce me to the clients, and we had so much leftover food she immediately thought of Trey and all the workers here."

Iris smiled and nodded her head. "That's so sweet."

Trey frowned. *Yeah, real sweet.* He looked over his shoulder and saw Donny getting ready to take his lunch break. Donny wouldn't mind. "Hey, Donny! Come on over here, will ya?" he shouted.

Donny lumbered over, smiling shyly at Iris, and then noticed Macie Jo.

"Donny, this young lady has brought you and the boys a feast. Will you give her a little tour and introduce her around. She's new in town." Turning to Macie Jo, Trey added, "I would love to, but I'm taking my girlfriend out to lunch."

He grinned at Macie Jo's astonished face and Donny's equal look of surprise. "Give me the keys, Iris," he ordered and then walked her around to the other side of the truck. Iris frowned at the distance between the ground and the seat.

"How the heck did you get yourself into this truck in that skirt?" Trey demanded picking her up by her waist and gently setting her on the seat.

Iris blushed and smoothed her skirt down. "I had to use a step stool and a chair. It really is restrictive, but I love the way it looks," she admitted.

And so do I, Trey thought with a grin. He walked back around to the driver's side of the truck and smiled as he saw Donny holding Macie Jo's hand as she tried to step through the gravel in her three-inch wedge sandals.

Chapter 13

Iris grinned at being taken to Applebee's. Riley would have rather died than be seen in a chain restaurant. He really was such a snob. Why had she never seen that before?

Trey held the door open for her and guided her toward the hostess. They were immediately seated, and she was glad because Trey's stomach was growling. The man was always hungry.

"What's good, Trey? I don't think I've ever eaten here," she said, casually looking through the menu.

Trey put his menu down, staring at her like she was crazy. "Who hasn't been to Applebee's? Are you even American?" he demanded.

Iris rolled her eyes. "Last time I checked. What's good?"

Trey grabbed her menu just as the waitress walked up to them. "Allow me," he said and then ordered for the both of them.

Iris shook her head at him. "It better be good," she threatened, trying to look mean.

Trey sat back and grinned lazily at her. "I know, I know, you have boots with my name on them. Look, I know women. You'd probably have ordered some dumb salad. But after what I saw back there, you deserve some serious protein. You're going to eat a hamburger that any biker chick worth her salt would be happy to devour. You stood up for yourself, Iris. It's time to celebrate the new mean, tough woman that you are," he said, sounding like he was proud of her.

Iris sat back and smiled to herself. "I did okay, didn't I?" She looked at him for confirmation.

Trey leaned forward and grabbed her hand, pushing the silk sleeve up to reveal her tribal tattoo. "I do believe that you earned this warrior tattoo. I am very proud to call you my girlfriend," he said sincerely.

Iris shook her head and crinkled her nose. "Your girlfriend. Like you would ever really date me."

Trey frowned letting go of her arm. "What do you mean by that?" he asked curiously. "Why would you think I wouldn't want to date you?"

Iris shrugged, feeling uncomfortable. She scanned the restaurant for their waitress. When she looked back at Trey, he was still waiting patiently for her answer.

"I'm not exactly the tough biker chick that you think I am. I'm really just a glorified interior designer. This is the real me. To be honest, I was kind of nerdy growing up. I read a lot and took a lot of art classes. I didn't even really date until I was in college. I'm not who you think I am," she said quietly, looking at him from under her lashes. "I want to be a tough, mean, crazy woman no one would dream of messing with, but I'm not. I'm just me."

Trey stared at her with a half-smile and looked charmed. "Well, I have to be honest, Iris. If I weren't a woman-free zone, and you weren't a man hater, you'd have to hire Donny to keep me away from you. I think you're the most beautiful, brave, amazing woman I've ever met. And you're actually a lot tougher than you think. Even without the boots."

Iris's cheeks turned pink and she smiled at him shyly. "Thanks. That's probably the sweetest thing a man has ever said to me. Too bad about that woman-free, man-hating stuff, huh?" she said, sounding a little regretful.

Trey nodded slowly. "Honestly, if it weren't for that invisible 'stay away' sign on your forehead, I bet you and I could be pretty amazing together."

Iris bit her lip, frowning, but was saved from making a reply by the waitress showing up with a huge hamburger and enough fries for three people. "There's no way I'll be able to eat all that."

Trey laughed and dug into his hamburger, not intimidated in the least. "Everyone says that, but then when it's all gone, they wonder where it went. I bet you a ride up to Deer Creek on my bike that you can eat at least half of that."

Iris had no clue what Deer Creek was, but she was determined to find out as she grabbed the hamburger, careful not to get any ketchup on her silk shirt. A half an hour later, she pointed proudly at her plate. "You are so taking me on a drive later."

Trey frowned at her empty plate. "But look how many fries you have left. I'll consider it. But you have to promise to kiss me next time we run into Macie Jo. I'm sorry but that woman scares me," he said with a shudder.

Iris frowned and swirled a french fry in a circle of ketchup. "So she's the southern beauty queen you were talking about that first day? I should have realized. She's actually kind of sweet, Trey."

Trey frowned. "Are you throwing me to the wolves? I'm shocked. And after everything I've done for you. My lips are still bruised."

Iris winced. "No! Of course not. It's just I don't understand why you wouldn't want to date her. She's so beautiful and nice. You two look like you were made for each other. She's a beauty queen, and you're, well . . . look at you," she said gesturing at him with a sweeping of her hand.

Trey laughed softly and then took a sip of his soda. "Forget the fact that my sister-in-law is guaranteed to have told her some heartbreaking story about Allison dumping me for Will. Forget that she more than likely showed up today out of pity. She's all wrong for me.

"You know when you're a teenager and you have this idea in your head of what you want and what you like? Well, most of the time, people grow up and what they like changes. What they want changes. It took me a while to grow up. I had it in my head that there was a certain type of woman for me. Now, I've finally realized that I've changed. My tastes have changed. What I want has changed. I don't want Macie Jo. I want someone completely different," he said, staring at her intently.

Iris swallowed and touched the condensation dripping down the side of her water glass as if it were fascinating. "But what about your woman-free zone? Is that for real or were you just teasing me?"

Trey looked like he was considering how to answer that. "I'm definitely a woman-free zone. For all women, except one."

Iris looked down at her lap and noticed the black fingernail polish was chipping on her index finger. "Who might that be?" she asked in a voice that cracked nervously.

Trey smiled and crossed his arms across his chest. "You'll figure it out eventually."

Iris smiled but felt sick, wondering who it could be. "But if there's one woman who you could love, who you could open yourself up to, I'm probably in the way. What if she sees me and thinks you're taken?"

Trey waved that away. "She's not ready yet. In the meantime, you and I can have some fun. We can protect each other from the dating jungle, ride my Ducati as much as possible, and scare innocent children with your tattoos. What do you say? Are we still fake boyfriend and girlfriend?"

Iris exhaled the breath she had been holding slowly. Trey hadn't been talking about her. For a second, it had seemed as if he were talking about being interested in her for real. Crazy.

"But you're too good-looking for me. I honestly don't know who will buy it," Iris said, standing up and grabbing her purse. "I've never dated someone prettier than me. It'll take some getting used to."

Trey shook his head in confusion. "Iris, honey, that henna has poisoned your brain. That, or it's affected your eyesight. I can promise you that everyone in this bar is wondering what a gorgeous woman like you is doing with a mutt like me."

Iris laughed and pushed him toward the door, not even minding when he opened the door for her and then grabbed her hand. "I'll try not to stare so much, but it will be hard," she admitted laughingly.

Trey opened the door to her truck and picked her up, holding her for a few seconds longer than necessary. "Iris, you're good for my ego, you know that?"

Iris smiled and sat back, full and happy, as Trey drove back toward Alpine. Why was it so easy to be with Trey and so hard to be with Riley? Riley insisted she had never made him feel loved. And here was Trey looking like she had just made him feel like a king. She sighed heavily and leaned toward Trey, resting her head on his shoulder.

"By the way, thanks for being there for me today when Riley showed up. I don't know if I could have survived that without you," she said softly.

Trey wrapped his arm around Iris's shoulders and pulled her in close to his side. "I promise to slay all dragons and idiots. Of course that kiss at the end was quite a surprise. To Riley, anyway. I had a feeling you were going to find some way to kiss me sooner or later. Tough biker chicks like you are known to be very aggressive when it comes to attractive men like myself."

Iris giggled in embarrassment and looked up to find Trey looking down at her, his eyes sparkling with laughter. "Well, you know me better than I know myself. But I can't regret that kiss. I wanted to make a point to Riley, and to be completely honest, I kind of enjoyed it," she said sounding surprised.

Trey laughed. "Kind of? Honey, you were made for kissing. Trust me."

Iris sat up and looked at him in surprise. "But Riley said . . ."

Trey held up his hand, silencing her. "But Riley nothing. Riley doesn't even know you. You'll see. Sometime this week, when you kiss me in front of either Macie Jo or my sister-in-law, hopefully both at the same time, you'll see what I'm talking about."

Iris sat back, leaning into his side again. "Hmm, okay. I guess it's only fair. Just let me know when. I want to wear my boots next time," she insisted.

Trey kissed the top of her head and turned toward home. "I wouldn't want it any other way."

Chapter 14

Trey watched Iris drive off in her truck and hoped she wouldn't need help getting out. He had almost been tempted to call it a day and spend the rest of the afternoon with her, but he had a four-way inspection in two hours and had to make sure everything was perfect. He took his radio out of this pocket and went to work. Sam was coming by later to do a walkthrough as well, and he didn't want big brother breathing down his neck.

But first things first. He found Big Donny laying pipe with his crew and motioned for him to come over. Donny pointed something out to one of his guys and then joined him outside in the sun.

"Donny, you are a good man to have around," Trey said, shaking the man's hand.

Donny looked embarrassed but pleased. "That jerk won't be bothering Iris anymore. If he comes back . . ." Donny let the threat hang.

Trey used his imagination and smiled at the picture he had in his mind. "I kind of hope he does, now."

Donny laughed but still looked a little scary. "Me too. But what's with the beauty queen, Trey? I'm here to lay pipe, not to give girl scout tours. I'm behind schedule now," he said sounding ticked.

Trey held his hands up. "I apologize, Donny. I'm truly sorry, but Iris was upset. Besides, I thought you'd love having a gorgeous woman like that all to yourself," Trey said, honestly puzzled.

Donny shook his head and looked at him like he was an idiot. "I'd gladly get behind schedule to give Iris a tour. Now that's a woman to get in trouble over."

Trey's eyes narrowed, and his smile disappeared. "If I catch you trying to give Iris any grand tours, you're going to get a pipe to the back of the head."

Donny stared back, not as intimidated as he should have been. "It'd be worth it," he said but then relaxed and grinned as Trey put his radio in his pocket and stepped forward.

"Relax, relax, I'm pulling your chain," he said when Trey tensed up at the comment.

Trey shook his head, knowing Donny was telling the truth. Iris was turning out to be a handful. And he thought he had problems with Will Carson stealing his women. Donny could trample him and all of Alpine too.

"It's a good thing we're friends, Trey. You found Iris first. I can accept that," he said, sounding a little more sincere this time. Trey sighed in relief and took out his phone.

"I am glad to hear that buddy, because the reason I wanted to talk to you is that you earned yourself two tickets to that concert you were telling me about last week."

Donny's face lighted up as he gave Trey the information. Trey bought the tickets on the spot from his phone.

"You know, if you and Iris don't have plans, I'd love to take her with me. Just as friends, of course," Donny said, trying to look as innocent as possible.

Trey glared at Donny and punched his arm. "One more crack like that and I give the tickets to the electrician."

Donny laughed and sauntered away, whistling something tuneless and full of glee. Trey shook his head in consternation. He'd have to watch Donny like a hawk. It was getting to be a full-time job keeping men away from Iris.

He spent the next half hour putting out fires and dealing with an inspector who showed up an hour earlier than planned. In the end, they passed inspection, and he immediately sent out texts to Rick, Sharon, and Sam.

Trey glanced at his watch and smiled knowing he'd be seeing Iris in less than an hour. He had stopped to talk to one of the framers when he saw his brother Sam drive up in a big black Ram truck. Trey grinned as his brother hopped out and headed his way. When Sam reached him, he pulled Trey in for the usual headlock. Trey did a quick reversal and had his arm around Sam's neck, ready to take him down, when he heard an impatient sigh.

The two men immediately stood up. Trey groaned inwardly and gave his brother a hard look. Sam shrugged and shook his head, refusing all responsibility.

"Acting like eighth-graders. You're business owners. Grown men, for Pete's sake," Sophie said shaking her head with a pinched look around her mouth.

Trey raised his eyebrows at her tone of voice and noticed that Sam had already abandoned him to talk to Donny. He sighed, shoving his hands in his pockets and preparing himself for whatever was coming.

"Macie Jo said you totally ignored her and left a minute after she got here. She said some giant dragged her around the job site, took the trays of food from her, and then practically ordered her to go home. What in the heck?" Sophie said, looking far meaner than Iris ever could.

Trey bit back a smile and tried to look contrite. "Well, if I were Macie Jo, I'd be furious with you too. Really Sophie, using your stylists to make deliveries."

Sophie huffed out a breath and tried to regroup. "She was here to meet you, Trey. She wanted *you* to give her a tour."

Trey stopped smiling. "Why?"

Sophie glared and kept up her assault. She was determined to help Trey whether he wanted help or not. "Because she's perfect for you, Trey. I know it. Everyone knows it. And if you'd just give her a chance, you'd know it too."

Trey's eyes turned a shade colder. "I believe I mentioned to you just the other day that I've already found the perfect woman. I don't want, or need, your help when it comes to my love life, Sophie. You need to stop." Sophie blinked in surprise. She had never been a witness to Trey when he was mad, let alone been on the receiving end of Trey's anger.

Sophie paused and thought carefully before she spoke. "I love you, Trey, like you're my own brother. I care about your happiness. It kills me to see you sad. But I'm sorry, you can't seriously be in love with Iris. I don't believe it for a second. No one in their right mind would buy it.

She is wrong for you. Wrong, wrong, wrong. I don't care what anyone says. A woman who would destroy her own beautiful hair and get tattoos is someone with some serious issues. You need a woman like Macie Jo. Beautiful, sweet, and *normal*," she said, stressing the word normal so much, she practically shouted it.

Trey looked up at the sky and counted to ten. "I know you love me, and that's why I'm going to forgive you for insulting Iris. But trying to sell me on normal when I can have her isn't going to work. Do I look like a man who wants to spend the rest of his life bored to death? Sophie, I'm only going to say this one more time. Leave it alone. This is none of your business."

Trey turned and walked away before he said anything he'd seriously regret. He heard Sophie kicking up gravel and sighing as she ran to catch up to him, her little frame eating up the distance with surprising speed. Refusing to look at her, he picked up his pace. She'd get tired after a while.

"Family dinner! My house, this Sunday. I insist that you bring Iris to meet your parents if you're so sure she's perfect for you," she said grasping the sleeve of his shirt.

Trey stopped and stared at Sophie. She thought she had him. He grinned wickedly down at his sister-in-law and took the challenge with relish. "I can't wait. We'll bring the salad," he said and left her in the dust.

Chapter 15

Trey waited until they were back from Heber before bringing up the subject of meeting his family. Iris had invited him in for a drink and had ended up calling for a pizza too. Trey sat on the couch, with Sally sitting at his feet begging for a pepperoni.

"Isn't she cute?" Iris demanded, picking all her pepperonis off her pizza and feeding them lovingly to Sally.

Trey grinned at the dog and threw a pepperoni high in the air, laughing when she caught it perfectly. "Yeah, she's all right for a cock-a-poo. She's no boxer or mastiff, but she'll do. Listen, Iris, I hate to bring this up, but remember that kiss you owe me?"

Iris glared at him. "Trey, I am an honorable woman. I promised I'd make it up to you, and I will."

Trey laughed and shook his head, "Yeah, well thanks to my sister-in-law Sophie, it looks like Sunday will be the perfect opportunity. *We've* been invited to my brother Sam's house for dinner so you can meet him and my parents. You up for that?" he asked watching her closely.

She didn't look upset, but as the seconds turned to minutes and she still hadn't said anything, he began to worry.

"It is a lot of pressure, isn't it?" Trey admitted.

Iris shrugged. "It's not that. I don't mind meeting your parents. After everything you've done for me and all of the motorcycle rides you've taken me on, I'd meet the president of the United States for you."

Trey felt his heart melt at her earnestness and gave in to his urge to run his hand down her hair. "Then what is it, sweetheart?"

Iris finally looked up at him and looked uncomfortable. "Well, it's your parents. It's one thing to pretend to be your girlfriend on the job site, or at a restaurant, but I don't feel right about lying to your mom and dad," she said biting her lip.

Trey sat back and frowned. She had a point. He didn't mind messing with Sophie, but his parents were a different matter altogether. His mom especially.

"Well, then we don't have a choice, Iris. From now until further notice, you're my real girlfriend and not my pretend girlfriend. After the dinner on Sunday, we'll reconvene and figure out our status."

Iris looked stricken. "Maybe you should call Macie Jo," she said petting Sally sadly. "She looks more the part. I mean, I know what my parents would say if I brought someone like Donny home for dinner. They wouldn't be happy at all. What will your parents think when they see my hair and my tattoos and everything? I wasn't exactly thinking of meeting my boyfriend's parents when I went a little wild and started making changes," she said gesturing toward her boots.

Trey put his plate on the side table and took both of Iris's hands in his. "I think you're perfect. I love your hair. Sorry, but I do. I absolutely love your hair. I've got a thing for your tattoos too. And your boots are the coolest boots in the world. Anyone who disagrees is either insane or blind. And if I hear one more person tell me that Macie Jo is the perfect woman for me, I'm going to do something violent," he vowed, meaning ever single word.

Iris's eyes widened in surprise, and then she grinned, her bright-green eyes sparkling. "You don't mind my new look? Really?"

Trey ran a finger up her arm, tracing the tattoo almost lovingly. "Not even a little bit, and I promise my family won't either. So, are you in?"

Iris laughed at Trey's puppy-dog face. "I'm in. Let's shake on it."

Trey shook his head. "Well, you're my official real girlfriend as of this second. I don't think this momentous occasion calls for a handshake."

Iris swallowed nervously and stood up to pick up their empty plates. She looked over her shoulder as she walked to the kitchen. "How about a hug?"

Trey shook his head again. "I don't think that'll be sufficient either."

Iris rinsed off the plates and put them in the dishwasher. "Um, what exactly did you have in mind?" she asked timidly.

Trey rose to his feet, feeling better and better about Sophie's dinner challenge. "Well, I think we should practice for the big kiss on Sunday. The kiss today was a good start, but I want everyone to take one look at us and just know that we're together. There's a certain vibe couples put off. It's this invisible force field that everyone senses. We've got three days to come up with that couple vibe," he said walking slowly toward her.

Iris nodded her head in agreement. "You're right. I never thought of it that way, but you're right. Maggie and Luke definitely have that. But how do you get that vibe?"

Trey stood across the counter from her and braced his hands on the fake marble surface. "Well, kissing, for sure. Not too much, but just enough so you get it right. Hugging every now and then. And of course, the security that comes from knowing that your heart is safe with me and that my heart is safe with you. It's trusting that when I look at you, you know that I'll never look at another woman the same way and that when you look at me, that I can tell that you'd rather be with me more than any other man in the world," he said softly, staring into her eyes.

Iris's eyes softened, and she sighed, her toes curling in her black boots. "Oh, I want that," she whispered fervently. "I've always wanted that."

Trey nodded and walked slowly around the counter, coming within a few inches of Iris. "I want that too," he said. He reached out a hand and cupped the back of her neck, leaning in toward her.

The doorbell and Sally's almost instantaneous barking made him pause right before his lips met hers. He growled impatiently. "I swear, if it's not a life-or-death emergency, I'm going to kill whoever just interrupted me."

Iris giggled nervously, putting her hand over heart as she scooted past him to walk toward the door. She opened the door with a bright smile but immediately lost it as she saw her ex-husband standing on her front porch. Riley Shelton was not giving up.

"Riley, what are you doing here?" she asked nervously, looking over her shoulder. Trey was walking toward the door, looking meaner and more dangerous by the second. "You should go. Really, right now," she urged.

Riley rolled his eyes and then stopped and stared hard at her. "What have you done to your hair!" he demanded, stepping closer to get a better look.

He looked her up and down, his eyes pausing on the silver T-shirt splashed with brightly colored Samurai swords and the faded, raggedy jeans. But his eyes paused the longest on her boots.

"Is this a joke?" he finally said, ignoring Trey's presence at her shoulder.

Iris frowned and shook her head. "No joke. It's just me," she said simply.

Riley laughed, a cruel, crushing sound that had her wincing and Trey rubbing her back comfortingly. "You? The most successful and talented designer I know and you're dressed like some low-class . . . biker's girlfriend. The only reason I chose you over all the other women I knew was because you were perfect. I could never find anything wrong with you. Not with your style, not with your personality. You were always perfect. I could never find a woman better than you."

Iris's shoulders slumped, and Trey immediately put an arm around her waist. "You never loved me, did you? You were just collecting me because I went so well with your upholstery."

Riley paused and looked at his feet for a moment. "I'm not going to answer that right now. I'm willing to put these changes down to the fact that you've just gone through a traumatic event. I realize that finding out about the other women on our wedding day was a hard thing to deal with. However, I think annulling our marriage was a huge mistake, but it's something we can get past if we want to. I'm here, Iris. I'm asking you for another chance. You know what kind of life I can offer you. I can give you everything you've ever wanted. Your life will be filled with beauty and travel and things that most people can only dream of. You know that's what you want," Riley said, sounding convincing and tempting.

Iris felt Trey's arm fall away from her waist and immediately missed the warmth. "Can you offer complete and total fidelity? Can you promise me that you'll never look at another woman, flirt with another woman, have an affair with another woman?"

Riley looked uncomfortable but looked her straight in the eyes and said, "Yes."

Iris shook her head. "I don't believe you."

Riley huffed out an impatient breath and put his hands on his waist. "But if I could make you believe me . . . If you could trust me again, would you come back to me?" he asked.

Iris stared over his shoulder at the Ducati motorcycle and frowned. "I don't want that life anymore, Riley. I don't want a life filled with things. I want a life filled with love. If I went back to you, I'd never be sure. I'd be wondering every night you were home late if you were with someone else. And every time you'd leave the room to take a call, I'd be wondering who you were talking to. And every time you took a business trip, I would wonder. It would slowly kill me, and I've realized recently that I like being alive."

Riley sneered and gestured toward Trey, who was standing in the shadows. "And you think he'll love you? You think he'll stay true to you? What a joke. No man will. Men aren't made that way. We're constantly on the prowl for the next chase, the next challenge. He's lying if he denies it. I'm willing to work on my commitment issues, though. I can't promise to be perfect. That's not possible, but I'm willing to try. I've been seeing a counselor lately to deal with everything since you left me. I've learned a lot, Iris, and I can't wait to prove to you how willing I am to do what I need to, to get you back."

Iris stood up straighter and shook her head. "No, I want more. I want passion, love, and complete faithfulness. Not because you have to, but because you want to." She paused and looked at the disbelief on Riley's face. "Please don't come back again. It's over. I've moved on. I'm dating a biker now. And he will run you over with his motorcycle if he sees you again," she said gesturing to the Ducati parked in the driveway.

Riley glanced at the motorcycle and turned back to glare at her. "You're making the biggest mistake of your life."

As Iris watched Riley walk away for the last time, she felt an easing in her heart. The last of her heartbreak seeped out and was replaced with peace. She felt Trey's arms wrap around her and pull her to his chest and sighed in contentment. "You didn't even say one word," she scolded.

Trey leaned down and kissed the top of her head. "I didn't need to."

Chapter 16

Iris spent the next three days running back and forth to the job site, showing samples to Rick and Sharon and ordering materials. Her little project was turning into a bigger and bigger project. She was determined to stay on budget, though, so she spent a lot of time calling old contacts and friends in the industry, getting seconds and returns.

The time she usually spent on the back of Trey's motorcycle taking mini trips up the canyons was now spent working late into the night. She felt good. She was busy doing the things she loved. And even though she wasn't spending as much time with Trey, he always seemed to find a few minutes every day to wrap his arms around her and tell her how beautiful she was. But the big dinner with his family was tomorrow, and she still wasn't sure what to do about it.

Trey acted like it was no big deal, but deep down, she knew, on a level that most women understood, that this was huge. That was why she told Trey that she'd be too busy to see him until the next day, when he'd pick her up after church. Today she was taking a special trip into Salt Lake to pick up a few things.

Since she had agreed to make the salad, Trey gave in easily and went off with Luke and Sam to catch the latest Robert Downey Jr. movie. She didn't get home until nine, but as she laid her purchases on the counter and put all the salad stuff away, she felt good about her decision. Trey deserved it.

Iris frowned to herself as she gathered her purchases and walked upstairs to her bedroom. She sat on her bed and thought seriously about the man she had grown so close to so quickly. She turned and looked in the mirror, sliding her hands through her hair and looking into the eyes of a woman who was definitely starting to fall hard for Trey Kellen. She wasn't completely stupid when it came to relationships, though. She sensed that Trey wasn't anywhere near a woman-free zone. But it was just too soon. What if she was on a rebound? What if Trey was on a rebound from Allison? What if this was just another big mistake she was making?

Iris groaned and lay down on her bed, pillowing her head on her hands. When it came down to it, did it even matter? Trey had been her friend and helped her out every time she had needed him. It was only fair that she do the same for him. And if she was starting to fall for him, well, she could just keep that to herself. At least for the time being. She felt a little better and began to hang up her purchases. She needed her beauty sleep if she was going to impress everyone tomorrow. She wanted everything to be perfect. Then maybe his sister-in-law would finally back off.

* * *

Trey drove his Ducati to Iris's house at exactly four o'clock. He prayed she knew what she was doing when it came to salads, but if it turned out to be a bag of iceberg and a bottle of ranch, he was willing to deal with it. Just having her show up to meet his family as his girlfriend was huge. She'd come a long way from the girl he'd met in the ice cream aisle at Kohler's. She'd been so burnt out on men that he was surprised she hadn't maced him. And now, she was even open to snuggling, hugs, and the occasional kiss. He grinned and wondered how they'd plan the big kiss scene for Sophie's sake. He honestly didn't care what Sophie thought one way or the other, but Iris was the best kisser he'd ever been with. Not that he'd ever let that information get out. He knew for a fact Donny would have no qualms about disposing of his body in order to take his place

He rang the doorbell and held the bouquet of dark roses behind his back. His eyes widened as the most beautiful woman he'd ever laid eyes on opened the door and smiled shyly at him. Her hair was pulled up in a clip with loose strands framing her face. Her makeup was restrained and expertly applied. The long-sleeved, button-down shirt she wore was tucked into a tasteful knee-length skirt that shouted class, sophistication, and money. The demure low-heeled sandals finished the effect perfectly.

"What have you done with my girlfriend?" he asked, frowning slightly.

Iris smiled and twirled in a circle for him. "Do you think your parents will approve?" she asked.

Trey nodded but hid his sigh of disappointment. He'd wanted his family to meet the interesting and colorful woman who had caught his eye. Now she looked just like every other woman in Alpine. She fit in perfectly. The clip hid her flaming hair, and the long sleeves hid her tattoos. She wasn't even wearing her boots. Trey smiled and gave her a quick hug. "The pearls are a nice touch, sweetie, but you didn't have to do this for me."

Iris frowned. "I know I didn't have to. But I wanted to. I spent hours making sure it was just right. I don't want anyone giving you a hard time because of me."

Trey smiled and hugged her tighter. "Well, then that's incredibly sweet of you. Here, stick these in some water so we can go," he said, bringing the roses from behind his back. Delight bloomed on Iris's face, making her cheeks flush and her eyes sparkle.

"You brought me flowers," she whispered in awe, as if no one ever had before.

Trey shook his head at the idiocy of some men and bent over to kiss her cheek. "The first thing that you need to understand about being my girlfriend is that you will be treated as a queen."

Iris sighed happily and smelled the blooms. "What did I do to get so lucky?" she said beaming at him.

Trey puffed out his chest, feeling like the best boyfriend ever, and followed her into the kitchen where she filled a vase with water.

"Uh, Iris, how's the salad situation? I have some stuff for a simple salad back at my house if you didn't get around to it," he said looking at the bare counters.

Iris motioned toward the fridge as she snipped the ends of the roses with scissors and arranged the blooms so they weren't clumped together.

Trey opened the fridge and saw at least twelve small plastic containers and a large, plastic-covered salad bowl with fresh spinach and field greens. He was impressed. He quickly took all of the containers out and looked for a grocery sack to put everything in.

"I've got it covered, Trey," Iris said, leaning to the side of the counter and picking up a professional looking tote.

"I love to cook," Iris confessed. "I've been on a vacation from cooking lately, hence the Hot Pockets, but I usually like to take a different cooking class once or twice a year. Remind me to make you some Thai food. My favorite," she said off-hand as she quickly layered the different containers inside the tote and then grabbed her truck keys. "With this skirt and the salad, it looks like we'll be taking the truck."

Trey took the keys from her and motioned her toward the front door. "Ladies first," he murmured, realizing that the woman he was getting ready to introduce to his family was definitely a lady and probably the most well-rounded, talented, beautiful, and kind woman he'd ever met.

Fifteen minutes later, Trey ushered Iris into his brother's house. It was a gorgeous beast of a home, situated on the top of a mountain between Alpine and Draper. It looked like it should be on the front of a magazine, and had been, at least twice that he knew of. The rustic materials and use of stone and wood was truly amazing. Trey's own house had been a home that he and Sam had built for a computer whiz who had backed out right before closing. It had suited Trey, so he bought it for himself. But he preferred Sam's. It was more his style.

"What do you think?" Trey asked, taking the tote from Iris and leading her toward the kitchen.

Iris was still looking around taking in all the details and storing them away in her mind. Trey grinned as he saw the interior decorator in her analyze the color, style, and overall effect. "Well, is it up to your standards?"

Iris sighed and stared out the large windows that looked out onto the mountainside and the Lake beneath. "I love it. I wasn't sure I would, but I do."

"Well, I'm so glad you approve of my home. I feel so much better now." A cold voice came from the doorway leading into the kitchen.

Trey frowned, glancing up to see Sophie with her arms crossed and a cold look in her eye. He caught her eye and raised his eyebrows, warning

SHANNON GUYMON

her to behave herself. Sophie ignored him and walked toward Iris, looking her up and down as if she were a specimen.

"Well you clean up real nice, Iris. The last time I saw you I think you were wearing ripped up jeans and biker boots."

Trey watched as the pleasure on Iris's face melted away leaving a cold, expressionless woman that had him stepping toward her in concern.

"Oh, I get it now. I've met you. You work at the salon. You were going to do my hair, but Macie showed up and did it instead," Iris said looking back at Sophie coolly.

Sophie nodded and continued her inventory of Iris from her shoes to her shirt. "Yeah, I just didn't have it in me to ruin your hair. Macie Jo told me later how interesting your hair turned out," she said looking pointedly at Iris's hair, mostly hidden in a twist.

Iris looked at Trey as if to say they were going to be even after this. Trey nodded silently, in full agreement.

"Hair is a fun accessory. I think it's important not to get stuck in a rut," she said, looking back at Sophie's hair and doing her own inventory.

Trey hid a grin and caught sight of his mother and father. "Mom! Dad! Come meet Iris," he called out, hoping his parents would neutralize his sister-in-law.

The two older people walked quickly into the foyer from the kitchen and formed a circle around Iris. Smiling and waiting to be introduced.

"Iris, this is my father, Stan Kellen. Dad, my girlfriend, Iris Levine," he said proudly with his arm around Iris's shoulders.

Iris smiled warmly at his father, ignoring his offered hand and going for a hug. "Stan, can I just tell you that I've been wondering where Trey gets his good looks. Now I don't have to wonder anymore."

Trey grinned as Iris charmed his father. She had one more hurdle, though. His mom. "Iris, this is my mother, Sue Kellen. Mom, my sweetheart, Iris Levine."

Iris turned toward his mother and just shook her hand. "Sue, I can't tell you what an honor it is to meet the woman who raised such an amazing man. When I see all the good qualities that Trey has, I know it's all because of you. Thank you," she said and then pulled Sue in for a long hug too.

Trey stood in awe as the two women finally pulled apart and his mom wiped a tear from her cheek. "Iris, that is the nicest compliment

I've ever received. Can I just say that I've been praying for Trey to meet a woman who appreciates the dear, dear man that he is. Looks like the Lord has finally answered my prayers."

Iris smiled and took Sue by the arm. "Please tell me every embarrassing thing Trey has ever done. Start at the beginning," she said, grabbing her tote in one hand as they walked into the kitchen together, leaving Stan and Trey looking at each other with twin smiles.

"Home run, son. Home run," Stan said and slapped his son on the back. They followed the two women out of the room to the back of the house, where Sam was busy entertaining Adam in the nursery. Trey looked over his shoulder at Sophie and smiled with relish at the look of shock on her face. Sophie had just met her match. Iris was not a woman to be messed with.

Chapter 17

Iris expertly crafted the salad as she laughed and talked with Sue. The two different cheeses and the scallions, radishes, olives, almonds, mushrooms, bacon, and sun-dried tomatoes had to be assembled just right to make the perfect impression. Food needed to look as good as it tasted. At least that was what Iris had been taught.

"I just don't understand why someone as gorgeous as Trey isn't already married," Iris said with a shake of her head. "I swear every time I look at him it's a shock to my system. He's just flat out beautiful."

Sue nodded her head. "Don't tell him this, but when he was a teenager, I was approached twice by modeling agencies. He'd rather get a touchdown any day over a shampoo commercial, though. So we never made an issue of it. I don't even think it matters to him."

Iris nodded in agreement. "You're right. But it's a good thing. If he realized, I don't think he'd be with me," she said with a laugh.

Sue frowned. "You're joking! You're so exotic looking with that dark hair and your green eyes. I think you're just as beautiful as Trey, honey. You're just visual opposites. Like yin and yang, dark and light."

"Good and evil," Sophie said cheerfully, walking into the kitchen.

Sue looked up at Sophie in shock.

"Oh, what are we talking about?" Sophie asked innocently.

Iris smiled blandly and wiped her hands on a kitchen towel. "Oh, just how gorgeous Trey is and how opposites attract."

Sophie sniffed lightly and pulled a casserole pan out of the oven. "That's true. I just think it's strange that Trey has been attracted to tall, beautiful blondes his whole life, and all of a sudden here you are. Right out of the blue," she said, shaking her head and looking perplexed.

Sue frowned at Sophie. "Sophie, are you feeling okay? You're acting a little out of sorts, dear," she said, her voice sounding a faint warning.

Sophie smiled brightly and turned away. "Never felt better, Sue! Let's eat."

Sophie, Sue, and Iris brought all the food out and then Sue left to call everyone to the table. Sophie stood on one side of the table as Iris stood on the other. Both women stared at each other, unsmiling.

"You're quite the bully, aren't you?" Iris finally said, breaking the silence.

Sophie's eyes widened in surprise at the accusation. "Not at all. I'm just very protective of the people I love. And you're quite the chameleon aren't you, Iris? Wild and out of control one day and the perfect little lady the next. It's almost like you're putting on a show. Like you're a fake," she said, staring Iris down.

Iris raised her eyebrows but didn't defend herself as Trey and Stan walked in, closely followed by Trey's older brother, Sam, who was holding a miniature of himself.

Trey motioned for Iris to come meet his brother. Iris immediately walked to his side, welcoming the comfort of his arm around her waist.

"Sweetheart, I want you to meet my older brother, Sam. He's a big fan of yours, and he's also your boss for the time being. Oh, and this is Adam, his son."

Iris looked up into the smiling, good-natured face of Trey's brother and smiled warmly back. "It's good to finally meet you, Sam. I'm so pleased to be working with you on this project. I can't get over how much fun it's been working with Rick and Sharon. Every sample and sketch I show them is like Christmas day," she said laughing with a shake of her head.

Sam grinned at her and nodded. "They call me every day to tell me how smart I was to get you on board. You're making me look good, Iris. I have to admit, I'm enjoying it. But Trey's been the brains and heart behind this project. I've taken a step back and given the reins to him. I think the two of you make a pretty great team," he said, slapping his brother on the back.

Trey grinned at Iris. "Luke's the one we should thank. He's the one who suggested Iris in the first place."

Iris ignored the shoptalk as she stared at the little boy. Adam, they called him. He was a perfect, little replica of Sam, except his hair was lighter. He smiled at her and reached out a hand. She looked up to Sam for permission and then reached out to the little boy, who immediately went to her as if he had known her forever. He patted her cheek and said in a high little boy voice, "Pretty."

Trey and Sam laughed and walked around the table, leaving her to hold the little boy in wonder. What would it be like to have a little boy like this? She felt a deep yearning grab hold of her heart, and she turned to look at Trey. He was looking at her with an intent expression on his face as he pretended to listen to what his father was saying. They stood there like that, just looking at each other as everyone bustled around them.

"I'll take him," Sophie said, grabbing her son out of Iris's hands and jerking her out of her trance.

Iris let Adam go and went to sit by Trey. He held her seat out for her and leaned down to whisper in her ear. "You're doing wonderful. After today, I think I might just give you my bike."

Iris looked up and laughed, knowing she'd get his bike over his dead body. Trey grinned and sat down beside her, immediately grabbing her hand.

Stan said the prayer over the food and everyone started talking and eating.

"So I googled you, Iris. I hope you don't mind," Sophie said with a sweet smile.

Iris looked worriedly at Trey, who was frowning darkly at his sister-in-law. "Um, I guess not. But why?"

Sophie laughed and pulled a roll apart for Adam. "Well, the way Trey has been talking, I figured somebody should find out a little about you."

Iris looked nervously at Stan and Sue who were looking at Sophie with consternation and embarrassment.

"I had no idea you were divorced," Sophie said, immediately looking to Trey to see what impact her bombshell would have on him.

Iris put a restraining hand on Trey's thigh as he flinched like he was going to jump up. Iris opened up her mouth to defend herself but closed it as Sam beat her to it.

86

"Sophie, I'd like to talk to you in the kitchen," he said, standing up and pulling Sophie with him. Sophie looked furious but followed her husband out of the dining room.

Iris cleared her throat, feeling mortified that her past was being thrown in her face in such an embarrassing way.

"Mom, Dad, it's not what you think," Trey said, sounding as angry as he looked.

Iris held up her hand. "Please, Trey, don't," she said, stopping him before he went any further.

"Stan, Sue, I'm not sure what's going on with Sophie or why she's decided to dislike me so much, but I think it has something to do with my hair," she said with a shaky laugh.

Sue blinked a few times and shook her head. "Please don't feel like you need to explain anything. Your personal life is your personal life. Stan and I have total faith in Trey's choice of companions. From what we've seen of you, you're a beautiful, kind, and talented woman," she said, sounding distressed.

Stan patted his wife's knee and looked pained. "We love our little Sophie to death, but she can be feisty at times. We all can. There's not a soul in this family that wouldn't do anything for Trey. And Sophie just happens to be very protective. You probably won't believe it, but one time our little Sophie got so mad at her own grandmother that she chopped her grandmother's hair off and dyed what was left a bright blue. Turns out she did it to defend her mom," he said with a laugh.

Trey didn't laugh. "If she comes anywhere near Iris with scissors or dye . . ." he said warningly.

Sue looked horrified and even Stan winced. "Yeah, you might have a point, Trey. We'll keep an eye on her. What were you saying about Sophie and your hair?" he asked worriedly.

Iris bit her lip but decided to stay silent as Sophie and Sam walked back into the room. Sophie held her chin high. Sam, embarrassed, looked Iris in the eye and said, "Iris, I'm sorry if you were embarrassed by Sophie bringing up your divorce. She was just trying to make conversation." He sounded doubtful.

Iris raised her eyebrows and looked at Sophie. Sophie shrugged and looked her in the eyes without any regret. "Sorry, Iris. I suppose it's not something you want to talk about in front of Trey's parents."

Trey shook his head in disgust. "It wasn't a divorce! It was an annulment for a marriage that lasted four hours. Get your facts straight, Sophie. Now since you're obviously determined to do this, since you haven't embarrassed Iris enough, get it off your chest. Once and for all, what is your problem? I've told you twice already to back off and leave my relationship with Iris alone. So go ahead. Out with it," Trey ordered.

Sophie looked to Sam for back up, but he held his hands up as if to say she was on her own. She huffed out a breath and lifted her nose in the air. "Fine. I will. Take your hair down, Iris. I dare you," she ordered coldly.

"Oh brother," Trey said tiredly.

Iris blinked a couple times but then lifted her hand to take the clasp out of her hair, letting the silken strands fall around her shoulders. Her hair that had recently been to her waist, now was three inches shorter. The subtle, natural shade of dark red enhanced the dark strands making it seem as if it were glowing in the light.

Trey immediately stood up and walked behind her chair, letting his hands run through her hair. "Why?" he asked softly, walking back to his chair. He ignored everyone else at the table and pulled her chair out, angling it toward him so she had to look him in the face.

"Iris, you loved it. *Why?*" he asked one more time, grasping her chin gently and lifting her face.

Iris bit her lip but then looked up, letting her heart into her eyes. "For you," she said simply.

Trey shook his head and then smiled so sweetly at her it almost hurt to see it. "You gave up your flame-tipped hair for me?"

Iris nodded just as Trey swooped in for his kiss. Iris was shocked, but then remembered she had promised to kiss him in front of everyone. She immediately forgot all about everyone else as she realized Trey didn't even care about that anymore. She'd never in her life been kissed like Trey was kissing her now. This was not for show. Trey wasn't trying to prove anything to anybody. He was just a man kissing a woman because he wanted to. There was tenderness, passion and, surprisingly, kindness. It made all other kisses fade away.

Sophie, loudly clearing her throat over and over, finally had Trey lifting his head. He grinned at Iris and then laughed as she finally opened her eyes.

"Oh, my," Iris managed, reaching up to touch Trey's cheek.

Trey grabbed Iris's hand and kissed her palm. "I will make it up to you, Iris. If it takes me the rest of my life, I swear I will. I can't believe you would sacrifice your hair for me," he said, shaking his head in wonder.

Iris cleared her throat, now really embarrassed as she sat up wishing her bones hadn't turned to butter. "Sorry, everyone," she said with a laugh, glancing around the table at everyone.

Sam was grinning at his little brother. Sophie looked disgusted. But Stan and Sue looked delighted.

"What else, Sophie? What else do you need to get off your chest?" Trey asked coldly, not forgetting about his sister-in-law sitting across from them, still glaring at Iris.

Sophie rolled her eyes. "Stan, Sue, I can see that you're buying this, but I'm not. This girl has some serious issues. She walks into my salon, wearing holey jeans, wanting her hair done like Katy Perry's, and then asking where she can get a tattoo. Is this really who you want with your son?"

Sue stared at her son and then at Iris. "Yes, Sophie. It is," she said simply and then took a bite of her salad.

Stan grinned at his son and shook his head. "So, did you really get a tattoo, Iris?"

Iris winced and undid the button on her wrist. "Actually, yes. I did," she said, pushing her sleeve up to reveal slightly faded tribal tattoo running up her arm.

Trey lifted her arm and kissed her wrist. "I'm getting one to match next week."

Iris grinned at him. "Really? You're kidding me," she said shaking her head.

Trey laughed and took out his phone bringing up his calendar. "Right there, the fifteenth at one o'clock. Brittany. Tattoo," he said grinning at her expression.

Iris gasped in delight. "I am such a bad influence on you."

Sophie made a harrumphing noise. "Exactly," she said darkly.

Trey looked coldly at Sophie. Sophie sniffed, still not ready to change her mind about Iris.

"Sophie, you've had your say. Now I'm going to have mine. Iris is my girlfriend and anyone who offends or intentionally hurts my girlfriend offends and hurts me. Do you understand what I'm saying to you?" he asked, staring at her, unblinking and unsmiling.

Sophie looked shocked and looked around the table for backup. Everyone, including her husband, looked grimly back at her. "Well, when everything falls apart, and you're left with a broken heart, just remember I told you so," she said, refusing to look at Iris.

Iris's mouth fell open, and she shook her head in wonder, saying, "I've never in my life seen anyone behave so badly. Maybe since you're so good at googling, you can google good manners and basic courtesy. Trey, I think it's pretty clear I'm unwelcome. Sam, I'm sure I'll see you at the job site. Stan, Sue, it was an absolute pleasure meeting you. Goodbye." She stood, allowing Trey to move her chair for her.

Before she could make her exit, Trey held her arm.

"Just to make things clear, Sophie, you and I are not good anymore. Sam, I love you, so I'm going to leave it at that. Out of respect for you."

Iris felt sick to her stomach at the waves of contention rolling through the room, but she walked out with her head held high and with as much dignity as she could find under the circumstances.

Trey's hand stayed on her waist as they walked quietly to Iris's truck. The sound of the front door opening and closing and running feet had them turning around curiously. It wasn't Sophie or Sam. It was Stan and Sue.

"Wait, you two!" Sue shouted, catching up to them. She paused to catch her breath. "I have a cheesecake in the freezer and enough ice cream to feed an army. Come over to our house and we'll have some dessert. Sophie doesn't speak for our family as much as she'd like to. Stan and I think you're delightful, and we couldn't be more pleased that you two are together. So let's just put this bad experience behind us, at least for today, and move on. The day is still young!" she said, sounding hopeful.

Stan nodded his head in agreement. "Actually, two bites of salad didn't do the job. Why don't I throw a few steaks on the grill and we can have a good, old-fashioned barbecue?"

Trey looked questioningly at his parents and sighed. "On one condition. No picking on my girlfriend," he warned.

Stan and Sue immediately promised to be as nice as possible. Iris laughed, feeling some of the tension ease. She and Trey followed his parents over the mountain to Draper and down the other side into a small, exclusive neighborhood.

"You know, that actually went far worse than I pictured it in my mind," Iris said, wincing.

Trey frowned and patted her knee. "You were amazing back there. You handled a fully loaded personal attack with grace and a lot of backbone. I couldn't be more impressed with you, Iris. And your hair . . ." he said, shaking his head and looking pained.

Iris scooted over and grabbed his hand in hers. "Think of it as token of my high esteem for you. I wouldn't have sacrificed my flames for just anyone, you know."

Trey looked at her like he was going to kiss her again, but she shook her head, "Keep your eyes on the road, buddy," she warned firmly.

"Not even for Donny?" Trey teased.

Iris leaned her head on his shoulder and sighed. "Not even for Donny. You know that sign I have on my forehead? The one that says, 'keep the heck away from me because I hate men'? It turns out there's one exception. You," she said simply, staring out the window and refusing to look at him.

Trey put his arm around her shoulders and held her close. "That is such a coincidence. Remember how I was a woman-free zone? Still am. Except for you," he said with a smile in his voice.

Iris smiled and snuggled in closer to Trey's side, feeling warm, safe, and happy. "What a wonderful coincidence. Too bad your sister-in-law is planning right this second to have me killed off," she said, not sure she wasn't kidding.

Trey was silent for a moment. "Sophie doesn't scare me. I'll just give Donny a call and let him know that Sophie was mean to you."

Iris laughed and felt better. It would work out eventually. Trey would make sure of it.

She spent the next three hours having a real family dinner at Trey's parents' house. When Sue took Iris on a tour of her flower gardens in the backyard, Iris decided to tell her about Riley and her annulment. She didn't want Sue to worry about any of Sophie's innuendos. She'd found that the truth was much better than gossip any day.

Sue surprised her by pulling her into a long, comforting hug. "Oh, sweetie. That is just so rotten. Heavenly Father must really want to make it up to you, because with Trey you've found the most faithful, loyal man on this planet. You will never have to worry one day about that boy, and you have my word on it," Sue promised, running her hands down Iris's hair.

Iris smiled and nodded. She believed her.

Chapter 18

ris walked around Maggie's studio the next day, picking out paints and brushes as Maggie decided on what size canvas she wanted her portrait done.

"I'm thinking we'll go medium. What do you think?" Maggie asked holding a canvas in her hand.

Iris looked over her shoulder. "I'd prefer bigger if you have one. I've already got an idea in my head, and I'll need the space."

Maggie smiled and immediately put the canvas down.

"So, how was the big dinner with Trey's mom and dad? I've met them a few times, and I'm always impressed with how relaxed and nice they are."

Iris picked up an angled brush and smiled sadly. "Oh, they're great. So sweet and accepting. It's just Trey's sister-in-law. I don't know if you've ever met Sophie Kellen, but I have to admit, I wish I never had."

Maggie slowly turned, her eyes narrowing as she studied the slump of Iris's shoulders.

"Didn't she like your boots?" Maggie asked quietly.

Iris let out a sound that might have been a laugh if it hadn't been so unhappy. "If only. No, I was on my best behavior yesterday. I wore a nice skirt and shirt. Very conventional, very boring. I covered up my tattoos, and I even cut my hair," she said, sounding almost weepy.

Maggie walked quickly over to Iris and put her hands on her shoulders. "I was wondering why you're wearing your hair up today. You're missing the flames, huh?"

Iris nodded, letting a tear slip down her cheek. "I made a salad too. I did everything right. I didn't want to make a bad impression on Trey's parents. I wanted him to be proud of me. But she was just so mean. I don't get it, Maggie. It's like she decided to hate me even before she knew me. Honestly, it was horrible. In front of everybody, she announced that she had googled me and that she knew all about my divorce. Right in front of Trey's family. During dinner! It was so cruel. Sam tried to stop her, but then she exploded about my hair and insisted I take it down and show everyone. I had to show them my tattoos, too."

Maggie's eyes were so bright with anger they glowed, but her voice was gentle. "Iris, what did Trey do? Did he stick up for you? Did anyone?"

Iris nodded her head, and as she wiped the moisture from her eyes, she turned to find a chair. She sat tiredly and tried to smile. "Of course. Trey was furious. You can tell he loves Sam so much, so he couldn't tear Sophie apart. But very respectfully he said that he wouldn't come back to her house again. Stan and Sue left with us. I had to leave, Maggie. I just couldn't stay anymore. She even told Trey that she knew I would break his heart. It felt like she was verbally going after me with a battle-ax. And I still don't understand why."

Maggie breathed in and out a few times before she answered. When she did, she sounded very calm.

"Iris, you have a good heart. I can tell. I think everyone can tell after five minutes with you that you're an angel. If Sophie has decided to not support your relationship with Trey, then she's the one who's missing out. And let's be honest, Trey's mad at her now, and she adores Trey. I bet you a million dollars Stan and Sue are furious with her. They want nothing more than for Trey to be happy, and you do that for him.

"The other day, when Luke got back from the movies, he said that it was like someone had turned on a light switch for Trey. And Sam. He's the most amazing older brother you can imagine. He loves Trey so much he'd do anything for him, so I can't imagine that he's very happy with Sophie right now either. I bet she's regretting the way she's acted."

Iris nodded her head and sighed heavily. "But it still hurts."

Maggie's face hardened and she looked down, shaking her head. "You just moved. You're working again. You've started a new relationship. So many good things. There's no reason to spend any energy worrying about some crazy woman who doesn't even know you."

Iris smiled and nodded. "You're right. I can choose to let her make me sad, or I can choose to be happy. I shouldn't give her so much power over me, huh?"

Maggie smiled and walked over to hug her. "Absolutely not. And you've been here fifteen minutes and haven't even once mentioned my new boots," she said chidingly.

Iris jumped up and covered her mouth with her hands in delight. "You really got them!"

Maggie modeled her custom sage-green biker boots for Iris and felt a thrill of happiness from the joy blossoming on Iris's face. "Honestly, wearing these boots makes me feel like I could conquer the world."

Iris giggled and threw her arms around Maggie's neck. "You are so right. And look, we match now. Just like good friends."

Maggie grinned. "Don't tell Luke, but I'm getting some henna tattoos done this week."

The sadness Iris had been feeling since the dinner party completely disappeared. "I love you, Maggie."

Maggie swallowed a lump in her throat and silently swore she was going to use her new boots for kicking a certain redhead's rear. "I love you too, Iris."

Maggie helped Iris carry the art supplies over to her house, but as soon as she was back home she called Allison and Jacie and told them to come over immediately. Sophie had broken the first and only rule. And for every crime, there had to be a punishment.

Chapter 19

Iris worked on Maggie's portrait for a couple soul-soothing hours and then spent another hour on the phone talking to distributors and catching up Rick and Sharon on all of the progress she had made. Most of the chairs and tables had been ordered. The light fixtures were being delivered next week, and she was going with Trey to pick out the flooring that afternoon. Plus, she had an appointment with the painter tomorrow morning, so she was caught up with everything.

As she washed the acrylic paint from her hands, she glanced at the clock and wished it would hurry up. She had to wait three more hours until she saw Trey. She smiled to herself as she dried her hands and admitted she had it pretty bad. Every time she saw his mischievous smile, her heart raced. But she refused to turn into one of those girls who waited by the phone or insisted on being glued to the hip. No way. She was a strong, independent woman who happened to have a life of her own. So what if she had started thinking of him constantly. She'd learned about it in one of her psychology classes. During the first stages of love, a person's brain reacted the same way it would as if it were on drugs. The same pleasure center of the brain showed activity when the two subjects were around each other.

She couldn't say what was going on in Trey's head, but there was a crazy, out-of-control party going on in her brain every time she even thought about him now.

Iris laughed at herself, but at the same time, accepted it and enjoyed it. At least she was mature enough to understand what was going on. She grabbed the keys to her dad's truck and decided it was time to get out of the house. On a whim, she decided to drive down to the Peppermint Place. Trey had pointed out the cute little candy store when he'd taken her on his Alpine tour. She was sure Talon could use a lollipop, and Maggie and Luke had been so kind and welcoming, she'd get them a thank-you treat too.

She parked her truck and walked in, pleasantly surprised by the store. It was darling, and they had almost every candy you could dream of. She took her time walking through, putting this and that into her basket. Pretty soon, she was buying candy for everybody she knew in Alpine. Trey was getting a big bag of chocolate-covered potato chips. She grinned, already anticipating his reaction. She even picked a treat for Donny, for helping her out with Riley. He really was just a big sweetie.

She turned the corner and reached for a bag of cotton candy when she felt a timid tap on her shoulder. She turned around, smiling, assuming it was a clerk, but found herself staring at a beautiful blonde woman who was looking at her anxiously.

"Excuse me, but would your name happen to be Iris?"

Iris put the bag of cotton candy down and smiled back at the woman cautiously. Who in the world would know her?

"Yeeees," she answered.

The woman cleared her throat and then looked down at her boots. "I was almost positive you were. I've heard so much about your boots from Maggie, I could probably pick you out in a crowded mall. I'm Allison Carson, by the way."

Iris's eyes widened as she realized who she was talking to. This was the woman who had broken Trey's heart. This was who he had been in love with. Iris nodded her head, taking in all of the details of the woman as she tried to smile. She was truly beautiful. Not in an in-your-face kind of way, but in a genuine, simple way. He hair wasn't big, her makeup was minimal, and even her clothes were basic. She wasn't trying to cram her looks down anyone's throat. Which made her all the more arresting.

"I can see why Trey had such a hard time getting over you," Iris said quietly, wondering if Trey really truly was over Allison.

Allison shrugged, looking uncomfortable by the compliment. "This is going to sound strange, but would you like to have lunch with me?"

Iris winced, thinking of a page full of things she'd rather do but knew from Allison's expression that it had taken a lot for her to offer the invitation. "Sure. What did you have in mind?"

Allison smiled as they walked to the counter. "My house, if that's okay. I'm not in the mood for fast food. We can talk while I throw a salad together."

Iris nodded and then paid for her purchases, wondering what in the world she had gotten herself into.

Iris followed Allison down a quiet street until they came to a three-story home that had Iris smiling in pleasure. It looked like a home from the Pacific Northwest. The style, the materials, and the way it almost melted into the trees were typical of the homes she was used to.

"I love your house," she admitted as she followed Allison into the foyer.

Allison grinned. "Me too. Will had it built before I even moved back to Alpine, but I wouldn't change a thing. I feel like I live in a fairy castle."

Iris smiled and walked over to a wall of photos. There were many pictures of two good-looking teenagers and a few of Allison and a tall, handsome man. "Is this your husband, Will?" Iris asked, pointing to one of the pictures.

Allison set her purse down and nodded, her face practically shining as she looked at the picture. "That's my Will. We've been married for almost seven months now."

Iris smiled. "You two look very happy together." She said, feeling bad for Trey. It would be hard to be in love with someone who didn't love you back and was perfectly happy being in love with someone else. She wondered what she would do if Trey decided that he was in love with Macie Jo. The sudden hitch in her heart was answer enough. It would kill her.

"Come into the kitchen so we can talk while I throw something together. I know this is probably weird. You don't know me, and I don't know you, but we know so many of the same people. I, um, heard that you started dating Trey," Allison said, looking at Iris to gauge her reaction.

Iris smiled and nodded, sitting at the counter as Allison tied an apron around her waist. "Yes, we just started seeing each other. And before you ask, yes, I know all about Trey's unrequited feelings for you."

Allison winced and paused before grabbing a salad bowl. "Awkward. Sorry, but it can't be helped. Is that weird for you?"

Iris laughed, as she started to relax. "It's kind of weird. You're honestly one of the prettiest women I've ever met, so I have to give Trey a break. Who could blame him for falling in love with you?"

Allison blushed at the compliment and opened the fridge, grabbing an armful of vegetables and lettuce. "That's very kind of you. But here I am, thinking *finally*, here's a woman who is prettier than me, more interesting than me, and someone who will keep him on his toes. Today is a good day, Iris. Today, I can stop feeling guilty about Trey, because he has you."

Iris felt all the weirdness disappear and grinned. "Oh that's sweet. Thanks."

Allison must have felt the atmosphere lift too, because she smiled as she chopped and cut the ingredients for their salad. "But there's another reason that I asked you for lunch. And that's Sophie Kellen."

Iris's smile disappeared. "Are you friends with Sophie?" she asked, looking around her casually in case Sophie was getting ready for a surprise attack.

Allison waved her knife in the air. "Well, I am, but please don't judge me by that. Sophie is actually pretty wonderful. I know you haven't seen that side of her yet, but I'm hoping you will."

Iris shook her head and looked out one of the many windows in the kitchen. "Allison, if she wants to apologize to me, she'll have to do it herself. Sending one of her friends to do her dirty work is kind of juvenile."

Allison laughed and started throwing everything in the bowl, not caring about the haphazard presentation.

"Are you kidding? Sophie needs to be taken out to the tool shed and spanked for the way she's been acting. Oh, no. I won't be apologizing for her. She'll have to crawl on her knees and do that herself. And she'd better be quick about it, because Maggie is this close to killing her," Allison said, holding two of her fingers together in the air.

"Wait. Maggie? You know Maggie? Did she tell you what happened Sunday?" Iris said, feeling open and vulnerable. She'd spent the two months after her wedding being gossiped about non-stop and found that she truly hated being talked about behind her back. Her trust in Maggie began to slip away.

Allison looked up and saw Iris's horrified expression and immediately held up her hands.

"No! It's not like that. That's one of the reasons I asked you to lunch. I'm going to try and explain this whole situation to you. Maggie doesn't gossip. Maggie protects. And that's what I'm here to do. Help her protect you. Now that Trey's finally happy and in love with someone truly amazing, there's no way I'm going to let Sophie destroy that, even if she does have good intentions. Trey's been through enough. He deserves a little happiness. Or a lot, by the looks of you."

Iris shook her head in confusion but followed Allison and the two plates she held over to the table by the nook window. The two women sat down and picked up their forks.

"Explain," Iris demanded, feeling unsure and strange again.

Allison sighed and motioned for Iris to start eating. "It all started when we got together at Maggie's gallery. There's four of us who like to escape there once or twice a month to hang out, eat, and talk. Well, Sophie and I thought it was time we did something about Trey. He was starting to worry us. He wasn't snapping out of his funk, so we decided to meddle. We came up with this bet. Well, not really a bet. That makes it sound trashy. It was more of a quest with a prize at the end. Sophie insisted she had the perfect woman for Trey, and Maggie insisted she knew the perfect woman for Trey. You. Well, neither one was backing down, so Jacie said whoever Trey picked, whether it was Sophie or Maggie, they'd win a prize. Maggie's was free salon services, and Sophie's was a portrait of her son. But there's only one rule. That when Trey made his choice, the other girl would have to back off. No interfering with Trey's happiness. Well, we all agreed to it, including Sophie. And Maggie informed us that Sophie broke the rule."

Iris's eyes were huge. "You have got to be kidding. Trey is going to find all of you and run you over with his motorcycle. Especially Sophie."

Allison nodded, looking guilty. "I know. And you can tell him, that's up to you. But please know that our motive was honestly to help Trey. We weren't meaning to hurt him or you or anyone. We just wanted to help Trey find someone he could love. We just wanted him to be happy."

Iris shook her head. "So Sophie broke the rule. What now? What was the punishment if anyone broke the rule?" she asked curiously, taking another bite of salad.

Allison huffed out a sigh. "Well, it's not like we expected anyone to actually break the rule. I mean, who would put their interests above Trey's? Okay, Sophie did. But we never came up with a punishment. So this is what Maggie and I and Jacie came up with this morning. By the way, you'll meet Jacie soon. She can't wait. But we think you should come up with the punishment. Since you're the one who was hurt by Sophie. Whatever you say, we'll accept and follow through. Unless it's really weird or violent."

Iris's eyebrows shot to her forehead. "You women are crazy."

Allison laughed, taking it as a compliment. "I know, but it keeps us sane if you know what I mean. A little crazy is good for the soul. So what do you think? Maggie was going to bring it up to you hypothetically and then take it from there. But me? I think you should know the whole story."

Iris nodded, pushing her sunflower seeds around her plate. "I don't even know what to say. How do you punish a grown woman for making another person feel horrible? I wouldn't even know where to start. I don't think my brain works that way," she said honestly.

Allison grinned. "Well then you're in luck, because Maggie, Jacie, and I have really bad mean streaks. We'll come up with the list, present it to you, you pick one, case closed. Sophie takes her punishment, she apologizes, and you and Trey live happily ever after," she said in satisfaction.

"Okay, I'll agree, but who's to say Sophie will just stand there like a good girl and take her punishment?"

Allison raised an eyebrow. "Have you met my friend Maggie? Nicest person in the world? Yes? Well, then you haven't seen her when she gets mad. You think Sophie is scary when she gets mad. No, Sophie can turn into a firecracker. Maggie can turn nuclear. Sophie will take it because she knows Maggie will take her brand-new boots and use them on her."

Iris laughed, getting a kick out Allison. "You know, if you had a leather jacket and biker boots, we could be good friends."

Allison giggled and looked delighted. "Maggie is taking Jacie and me to the store you both got your boots at and we're getting some too.

I can't promise I'll get a leather jacket or change my hair, but I've definitely joined Team Iris."

Iris laughed, feeling 200 percent better. "Team Iris. Maybe I'll order T-shirts."

Allison considered and nodded. "Brilliant. I'll text Maggie and let her know. She'll design them."

The two women laughed and enjoyed talking for the next hour, finding they had a lot in common. Even past men troubles. Allison told her about her broken engagement to a man with a wandering eye.

"He married one of my best friends and they're already divorced. She caught him with their real estate agent."

Iris felt a little better knowing she wasn't the only one. "Why are men like that? Why wasn't I enough? Why weren't you enough? I don't get it," she said, honestly wanting to know the answer.

Allison pushed her plate away and put her napkin on top. "We are enough. I think we're both amazing. But the problem is, this world we live in. Over two hundred channels to choose from. Whatever restaurant they want. Clothes, shoes, cars, homes. We're raised on variety. And if we get bored, we drop it and move on. Men are raised on a steady diet of change.

"And then there's pornography. That usually goes hand in hand with cheating. That's why it's so incredibly rare to find a man who has stepped away from what the world tells him to want and decides for himself what he wants. I was very lucky. Will is someone I will never have to worry about. I know Trey's like that too."

Iris nodded, feeling her heart warm at just the mention of Trey's name. She glanced at the clock and squeaked. She was late meeting him at the job site. She quickly hugged Allison, wrote down her number, and thanked her for lunch as she ran out the door.

Iris drove quickly to the job site and winced as she saw Trey standing next to his bike, glancing at his watch.

She ran to his side, and threw her arms around his neck. "Sorry I'm late, gorgeous. Forgive me, please, but I just had the best lunch with Allison."

Trey's impatience melted off his face leaving a wary expression. He slowly removed Iris's arms from his neck and looked down into her face.

"And what exactly did you discuss over this lunch?" he asked, looking stoic.

Iris wrapped her arms around his middle and leaned her head on his chest. "Oh, the usual. Ways to punish Sophie. A bet four women had on who could come up with the perfect girl for you. Just boring stuff."

Trey groaned and motioned for the truck. "We're late; no bike ride for you now. And you have a lot of talking to do," he said.

Iris laughed but hopped back in the truck, refusing to give Trey the keys this time. She revved the engine a little bit louder than she should, but she enjoyed it. Trey gave her driving instructions and then sat back. As she drove, Iris gave him the rundown on the bet and watched from the corner of her eye as Trey grew quieter and quieter. She started to rethink her decision to tell him everything when he finally spoke.

"I didn't know Allison cared one way or the other. Interesting," Trey murmured.

Iris came to a red light and turned her head to glare at Trey. "That's the only thing you can say? You're delighted that Allison cares about you? Oh, that's just great. That's just perfect," Iris said in a deadly voice.

Trey grinned and looked out the window. "I guess I shouldn't enjoy the fact that she's been tortured over my misery. But I do."

Iris hissed out a breath and looked straight ahead. She wished she were limber enough to lift her boot and kick him with it. But in her jeans and with him sitting so close, it was physically impossible.

"She is incredibly beautiful," she finally managed, feeling her face getting red as she felt a nauseous fury.

Trey started playing with her hair as he slipped his arm around her shoulders.

"She is, if you like blondes."

Iris closed her eyes for a second and then pulled her truck to the side of the road. She was somewhere on Main Street in American Fork, but she didn't care. She hopped out of the truck and started walking. She couldn't be anywhere near Trey right now. She would either kill him or burst into tears. Both options weren't acceptable.

"Hey! Wait up!" Trey yelled, jumping out of the truck and following her.

Iris ignored him and kept walking, kicking a stray soda can. Noticing a pawn shop, she yanked the door open and went straight to the clerk.

"Do you have any large hunting knives?" she asked in her most professional voice.

The grizzled older man with a goatee grinned and walked over to a glass case just as Trey banged through the door. Iris ignored him and walked quickly to the case.

"Show me this one," she said pointing to the deadliest and the largest. The man pulled it out and handed it to her just as Trey reached her side.

"Iris . . ." he began but shut up as she turned with the knife in her hand. She looked at him questioningly.

"Iris, if you'd have just stayed in the truck and let me finish what I was saying, you would know that since I've fallen for a girl with Cherry Coke–colored hair, blonde hair now bores me to tears. As beautiful as Allison is, she doesn't compare to you. If you'd have just waited a second, you'd probably hear me say something like, 'I'm so glad I'm over Allison now, because you're the only woman in the world I want to be with.' Now, put the knife down so I can kiss you."

Iris glared at him, tapping her right boot on the floor. She studied his serious face and then glanced at the knife. The man behind the counter looked fascinated. She held the knife up to the dim light. "Have I mentioned that since I'm a strong, wild woman these days that I might get jealous at the thought of you still having feelings for someone else?"

Trey inched closer, touching her boot with his. "From what I know about wild biker women, they do get in a lot of bar fights over their men. Some of them will even go to jail to prove their feelings. Lots of hair pulling, scratching, and the occasional baseball bat. But not too many use knives," Trey said, the left side of his mouth lifting, as his eyes sparkled.

Iris smiled and put the knife down on the counter. "Wrap it up. It's a present."

Trey grinned. "For me?" he asked, rubbing his hand down her arm.

Iris pulled out her wallet and slapped her credit card down on the counter. "No. For Donny. I just want you to know that he has it, in case you ever want to tell me how beautiful Allison is again."

Trey tipped his head back and laughed and then picked her up, swinging her around twice before setting her down. "I promise to never again mention Allison's beauty. I would never hurt you that way," he said more gently, kissing the side of her neck and completely ignoring the store clerk.

Iris pushed on his chest, making him look at her. "I really wasn't going to hurt you, I promise," she said, pushing a lock of hair off his forehead.

Trey grinned. "Don't ruin it for me, Iris. Having a woman like you go wild with jealousy over me has just made my life. Now be quiet, so I can kiss you."

Iris smiled as Trey swooped in, but instead of kissing her like he had before, it was different. It was slow and painfully more tender. She was shaky when he finally pulled away. And Iris knew that if Trey ever broke her heart, it would take more than a change in clothes and hair and a move to a distant city to get over him. She knew that there would be no getting over Trey Kellen. She had completely fallen in love with him.

Trey grabbed the knife, carefully wrapped in a bag, and hustled her outside. "Shall we forget the tile today and head back for my bike? I suddenly feel like playing hooky with you."

Iris grinned at the thought. She'd never in her life played hooky. Well, she was on vacation. It was time to try new things.

Chapter 20

Trey called and rescheduled with the tile company while she drove back to Alpine to get his motorcycle. Trey insisted that they grab her leather jacket from her house. "This field trip is on a bigger scale, and I don't want you getting cold," he explained. "I'm taking you to Park City for a real date." Iris let out a whoop and jumped up and down.

Before leaving town, he surprised her by stopping by his house to get his own leather jacket. For some reason, she was surprised he had one.

Trey's house was a gorgeous black-and-white, two-story craftsman-style home. Large front porch, large yard, but no trees, or bushes, or even grass.

As Trey opened the door to his house and let her in, Iris stopped smiling. White walls. Beige tile. No furniture. She silently walked past the living room into the kitchen. No kitchen table, no chairs. Nothing but two barstools. She bit her lip and walked into the family room. One black leather recliner and one flat-screen TV. No pictures. Nothing.

Iris turned and stared at Trey in horror. He looked slightly embarrassed as he held a brown leather jacket in his arms. "I haven't exactly gotten around to decorating."

Iris shook her head and opened her mouth to say something, but then shut it again. She had no idea what to say.

Trey slipped his coat on and walked over to stand right in front of her. "Before you make any harsh interior decorating judgments, I want you to consider something. This house is a blank canvas. It's been waiting for you, just like I've been waiting for you. Help us, Iris. Don't condemn us."

Iris laughed. "Blank canvas? Now you're just tempting me."

Trey wrapped his arms around Iris's waist and pulled her close. "Admit it, with your jealousy issues, would you really like some other woman's personal style all over my home? Hmm?"

Iris grinned wickedly and looked up into Trey's eyes. "You have a legitimate point. I'll start tomorrow."

Trey smiled in satisfaction and pulled her out of the house. "Excellent."

Iris was in heaven seeing all the fall colors in the canyon from the back of Trey's Ducati. An hour later, they reached Park City. The urban, chic feel of the town reminded her a little of home. The old-fashioned storefronts hiding glamorous offerings inside had her smiling with curiosity. Trey pulled up in front of a large hotel and handed the keys to his Ducati to a valet. Iris glanced down at her distressed jeans and boots and wondered if they were too underdressed.

Trey saw her wince, but grabbed her hand and pulled her inside. "This is Park City. Everyone from around the world comes here to relax. You'll see movie stars, billionaires, and bums like me having dinner in the same restaurant. And most of them look just like us. That's why everyone comes here. It's fun, relaxed, and the food is amazing."

She expected to see the maître d' sneer at them but relaxed when they were treated with friendly smiles and were seated immediately.

Iris devoured the menu with her eyes. This wasn't Applebee's. She didn't know which entree to pick. They all sounded perfectly amazing.

Trey smiled at her expression and put his menu down. "You know, it's only fair that since I insisted on ordering for you at Applebee's that you order for me tonight."

Iris looked up in surprise but loved the idea. "How fun! I promise I won't let you down."

Trey signaled the waiter to bring them drinks while Iris spent fifteen minutes making her selection. She frowned when she realized how expensive the restaurant was. She cleared her throat nervously. "So, gorgeous, what would you think about me buying you dinner tonight? You treated last time. It's my turn."

Trey blinked in surprise and then frowned across the table at her. "My dear Iris, are you worried that I might not have enough in my wallet to cover the tip?"

Iris blushed and felt embarrassed, but at the same time, she didn't want him to spoil her if he couldn't afford to.

"Let's be honest. This meal could easily run over a hundred dollars. You work for your brother and you have no furniture. Money's not exactly an issue for me, so just let me spoil you this time. You can grab the check next go 'round."

Trey sat forward in his chair, pulling the menu from her and grabbing her hand to kiss her knuckles. "Iris, honestly, it's sweet of you to worry about my finances, but to be blunt, I can cover the check and the tip. I don't work for my brother, we're partners. I own half of Kellen Construction. I bought my house two months ago and I've just been too busy to worry about the furniture. I'll give you my credit card tomorrow and you can go crazy decorating it to your heart's content. And if you're still worried, and I can tell you are, my father's family owns a successful publishing company out of California. I have a trust fund that will keep me and my children happily in the black for years and years to come. Now will you just order our dinners before I starve to death?"

Iris stared at Trey in surprise. "Really? But you seem so . . . so *normal*. You don't act like the wealthy people I know. You don't flaunt it at all. Besides your motorcycle, everything from your clothes to your boots is kind of worn."

Trey shrugged. "I like to be comfortable. We were raised knowing that we were very blessed. We're expected to help other people, to be charitable and grateful for what we have. My mom would tan my hide if she even thought I was prancing around flashing my cash. We live modestly and use what we've been blessed with responsibly. Sam takes it very seriously. Last year, he supported four young men from Alpine who didn't have money to go on missions. He finds who needs help and then does what needs to be done. I'm trying to follow his example."

Iris was intrigued and impressed. "And what about you? How do you deal with *noblesse oblige*?"

Trey looked uncomfortable but excited at the chance to talk about it. "Wells. Fresh water. Did you know that it takes some people in Africa hours just to carry water to and from their villages? I started a foundation to dig wells for whoever needs it. I get as many volunteers as I can find and we go over every summer for a month and do as much as we can. I went three months ago, and we dug wells for eight villages. Best experience of my life. I've got pictures back at my house I can show you. The little kids are the sweetest."

Iris held his hand as he talked. She made him pause so she could order their entrees but let him talk throughout the entire dinner. His eyes were alive, and the joy he felt from serving was palpable. As she listened, her eyes filled with tears and she wished with all her heart that she could have been there at his side.

Iris ordered braised short ribs with a Thai basil potato puree for Trey, and for herself she ordered smoked sweet potato soup with pork cheek and a cilantro lime cream sauce. She savored her meal, but she wasn't sure Trey even noticed what he was eating. When he paused to take a sip of water, she decided to ask. "Can I come next time?"

Trey's face brightened. "Of course you're coming. I was already planning on it."

Iris felt happier than she had in her entire life. She could see her future, and Trey would be in it.

The ride home went by too fast. It was getting late, but she didn't want to let go of Trey. She was trying to figure out a way to ask him inside as he pulled up to her house when she noticed lights on. Lights she hadn't turned on. She hopped off the bike and handed Trey her helmet.

"Trey, I think there's someone in my house. Will you come in with me?" she asked, sounding worried.

Trey grinned and took his helmet off. "I had a feeling you were going to find some way to get me to stay. You are one aggressive woman, Iris. Turns out, I absolutely love that about you."

Iris kicked him lightly with her boot. "Listen up, gorgeous, this isn't about kissing. I didn't leave those lights on. Seriously. Do you still have that knife?"

Trey stopped grinning and turned to look at the house. "I'm not the type of guy who needs a knife. Stay here," he ordered and walked quickly to the house.

Iris did exactly what she was told. She might be tough, but she was nowhere near stupid. She watched as Trey walked right through the front door without even pausing. He obviously had no qualms about fighting unknown intruders. It was almost as if he were looking forward to it. She had to admit, she was kind of impressed.

Two minutes later, Trey escorted two people onto her front porch. It was dark, so she couldn't see how badly Trey had injured them. She reached for her cell phone to call 911. This day was just too crazy.

"Iris?" Trey called out. "Come over here, honey. You have guests."

Iris paused and put her phone down. She walked toward the house feeling nervous. Who in their right mind would just walk into a person's home uninvited? No one except her parents.

As Iris realized who it was, she squealed in excitement and ran the rest of the way, jumping into her dad's arms. Everyone said he looked and acted like James Garner, but she could never see it. He was just her dad. He held her tight for a long time before finally letting go so her mom could hug her too.

"You didn't tell me you were coming!" she said, hugging them both again.

Noticing Trey standing in the shadows, Iris immediately went to him, pulling him into their circle. "Mom, Dad, this is my boyfriend, Trey Kellen. The bravest, best-looking, kindest man in the whole world."

Harris Levine nodded stiffly, his dark eyebrows forming a V. "Yes, we made his acquaintance as he burst through your front door, Iris."

Iris frowned and looked at her mom, whose friends insisted she looked like a modern-day Jackie Kennedy. She looked just as cold. "What? Oh! We thought you were burglars or something. Trey told me to stay outside while he made sure everything was okay. You didn't hurt them, did you?" she asked with a nervous laugh.

Trey frowned and shook his head slowly. "No violence. I promise."

Harris Levine reached out for his wife's hand. "We wanted to surprise you, Iris. It's late, so we're going to head back to our hotel. But we'd like to meet your for breakfast or lunch tomorrow."

Iris frowned, looking back and forth between her parents and Trey. "Um, I have an appointment with the painters tomorrow morning for the restaurant, but I'm free after that. Let's do lunch. Trey, did you reschedule the meeting with the tile distributor?"

Trey nodded his head. "Tomorrow at three."

Iris smiled. "Perfect. Let's just meet up at Thanksgiving Point for lunch tomorrow at noon. "

Harris and Rachel Levine kissed and hugged their daughter one last time before walking to their rental car parked in front of Luke's house. They hadn't bothered saying good-bye to Trey.

Iris frowned, feeling strange undercurrents. She held out her hand for Trey, who immediately twined his fingers with hers.

"Well, that was awkward for everyone. What happened when you came in the house, Trey?" she asked, as she pulled him through her front door and into her family room.

Trey sat down heavily on her couch and looked embarrassed. "I walked in, expecting Donny or Riley or some hoodlum, and instead there's these two older people sitting on your couch, drinking glasses of water. They looked at me like I was the intruder. Your father jumped up and threatened me with police brutality if I didn't leave. I quickly reassured him that I wasn't an intruder and that, in fact, I was dating the woman who lived here. That seemed to make things worse. Your mom stood up and said something like, 'Harris, this is worse than I thought.' By then, I knew I was in over my head, so I came outside to get you. Iris, this may come as a shock to you, because it's a total shock to me, but your parents don't like me."

Iris's mouth fell open in surprise and then she laughed. "Oh, wow. This is going to be fun," she said, collapsing on her couch with giggles.

Trey continued to frown at her and waited patiently until she regained control. "You know you're coming to lunch with me tomorrow," she said with tears of laughter seeping out of her eyes.

Trey looked horrified and shook his head quickly. "Not on your life. I would slay dragons for you. I would gladly run over your ex-husband. But there's no way I'm going to sit through a meal with two people who have taken an immediate and, might I add, unwarranted dislike of me."

Iris just grinned at him and took his large hand in hers. "I only have one thing to say to that, gorgeous. Sophie Kellen."

Trey groaned and fell on his side on the couch. Iris laughed again and stood up to walk into the kitchen. "Remember that whole boyfriend/girlfriend thing you came up with, Trey? I help you, you help me? Looks like you're up to bat."

Trey rubbed his hands over his face and stared at the ceiling. "I think you just played me."

Iris laughed and opened the freezer, pulling out two Chunky

Monkey cartons. "You have to admit, it's kind of funny. These people in our lives, who love us and want to protect us, for some reason, hate our choices in companions. What's weird is that I can sort of understand where Sophie is coming from. Here I am, a wild and crazy woman with the coolest boots in the world. I might come off as a little intimidating. But you? What could my parents possibly find not to like? You're sweet and kind and smart and practically perfect," she said, handing him a carton and a spoon before joining him on the couch.

Trey leaned over and kissed her cheek and smiled. "Have I mentioned how good you are for my ego?"

Iris shrugged. "It's the truth."

Trey took a bite of ice cream and relaxed. "Well, if we look at the situation logically, I'm guessing Riley high-tailed it home and immediately ran to your parents. He probably told them that you've fallen into the evil clutches of some biker who forced you to change your hair and buy a leather jacket. He gets your parents all upset and worried and here they are. Then I show up in my boots, leather jacket, and Ducati with their beloved daughter in tow and confirm everything Riley told them. Granted your hair looks flame-free now, but your black leather jacket and your boots and jeans are probably not what they're used to seeing you in."

Iris nodded her head. "That's it exactly, Trey. Now you're the big bad wolf. You're the crazy biker who has taken advantage of my broken heart to corrupt me and pull me over to the dark side. Oh my heck! I love it," she said with relish.

Trey looked at her and grinned. "You crack me up. Here I am getting ready to be eaten alive by your parents and you think it's the greatest thing since Chunky Monkey."

Iris smiled and snuggled in closer to Trey's side. "Do you think there's any way we can lock my parents in a room with Sophie for an hour?"

Trey laughed and thought seriously about the logistics. "Probably not. But you're welcome to show her the photographs of my dead body after your parents are through with me."

Iris rolled her eyes. "You're exaggerating. Relax. My parents are the best. You'll love my dad when you get to know him. He's so smart and funny. And my mom makes the best crepes in the world. You'll think you're in heaven when you taste them."

Trey snorted and took a bite of his ice cream. Iris frowned. "What?"

Trey shook his head. "That's assuming they figure out I'm not the big bad wolf. Until then, it's the end of a shotgun for me."

Iris shrugged. "I have complete faith in your ability to charm and delight anyone. Heck, I hated men, and I was your girlfriend hours later. That's skill."

Trey grinned and took Iris's ice cream out of her hand, setting it next to his on the coffee table. "Well, if I'm going to convince your parents that I'm Prince Charming and not the evil wolf, we better get working on our couple vibe."

Iris grinned and threw her arms around Trey's neck. "We really should practice."

Trey leaned back before Iris could kiss him. "Now, know your limits, Iris."

Iris looked slightly disappointed. "Fine, just give me five minutes of the best you have."

Trey laughed and pulled Iris closer. "You are the most interesting woman I've ever met."

It turned out that Iris did have a problem knowing her limits. Ten minutes later, Trey shook his finger in her face and left, promising to be there for lunch the next day.

Iris shut and locked the door and then headed upstairs. If she was going to sell Trey to her parents, she'd have to plan a strategy. She opened her closet doors and frowned at her clothes. She pulled out a silver-gray cashmere sweater and a pair of sleek, black Calvin Klein pants. Her conservative black heels were next. Then the hair. Her hair was classic, but she wanted to portray a little romance. She'd get up early and put her hair in curlers, maybe she'd pull it up on top, letting the waves and curls fall around her shoulders and face.

Iris got everything ready and then went to brush her teeth. She had thought that just bad relationships were complicated. It was a surprise to find that good relationships were crazy too.

Chapter 21

ris showed up at the job site to meet the painters right on time. Seeing Trey talking with the sheet rockers, she waved and kept walking toward the three men wearing white and waiting for her by the front entrance.

The meeting lasted longer than she anticipated. The head painter, Gerald, tried to sell her on a faux finish, and they had to battle it out. Finally agreeing on a color and texture, they shook hands. Iris glanced at her watch and groaned when she saw it was already eleven thirty. She noticed Trey standing politely to the side waiting for the painters to leave.

She hurried over and kissed him on the cheek. "You don't look like you're ready for lunch," she said noticing the jeans and flannel shirt he was wearing.

Trey smiled and ran his hand down her cashmere-encased arm. "This is me, sweetie. I'm not going to put on a suit for lunch. I think it's important that your parents realize that I'm not a suit-wearing, corporate kind of guy. I want them to know the real me."

Iris pouted for a second. "Well, of course I want them to know the real you. I adore the real you. But I dressed up for your parents," she said, wheedling.

Trey ran his finger through one of her curls and smiled down into her eyes. "Yeah, but I didn't want you to. I loved your flaming hair and boots."

Iris smiled and wrapped her arms around Trey's waist. "I love that you loved my hair."

Trey grinned and kissed her quickly. "So, it looks like you're playing dress up again."

Iris winced and stepped back so she could twirl for him. "I know. It felt weird putting my old clothes on. It doesn't feel right anymore. This is how I used to dress all of the time. This is what my parents are used to. I figured that it would put them at ease and maybe they'd give you a little break."

Trey sighed. "You're protecting me again? Iris, you have to stop sacrificing the real you for my sake."

Iris huffed out a breath and looked up at the ceiling. "You're right. This really isn't the real me. The real me is boots and T-shirts and jeans."

She shook her head and then smiled brightly at him. "This isn't the real me."

Trey laughed and grabbed her arm, leading her out of the restaurant. "Sweetheart, did you even have a doubt?"

Iris laughed and skipped toward her dad's truck. "Do you think I have time to change?"

Trey jumped in the truck and took the keys from her. "No. But you might have a point about your parents relaxing when they see the cashmere. We can get them used to the new you slowly. A tattoo one week. Maybe red streaks in your hair the next."

Iris laughed and tweaked her silk scarf back into place. "Wise, Trey. Very wise. Just another one of your amazing qualities."

Trey drove out of the parking lot and waved to a few guys. "And by the way, in case I haven't mentioned it, you look incredibly beautiful."

Iris shook her head in a confused smiled. "I thought you didn't like it when I dressed up?"

Trey glanced at her before stopping at a red light. "That day when you met with Rick and Sharon for the first time? I couldn't even speak for a good half hour. Today? Let's just say it's a good thing I know you so well, because if I didn't, I'd be too nervous to even talk to you. You're stunning."

Iris blushed and smoothed the crease in her pants. "I'm confused. I thought you liked my boots and jeans and crazy hair."

Trey grinned and grabbed her hand. "You're a beautiful woman in anything. But I live to see you in your boots and jeans, because you're so happy when you're in them. When you're happy, and getting a kick out of your boots, or enjoying your hair, there's no one in the world I'd rather look at."

Iris sat back and stared at the side of Trey's face, memorizing every angle, curve, and crease. "Would it freak you out if I told you I love you?"

Trey whipped his head around and stared at her. He stared until cars started honking behind him and he was forced to drive, but every three seconds he turned and looked at her. The silence went on for five minutes, but Iris didn't mind. Trey finally pulled into a convenience store parking lot and turned the truck off. He looked at her, his face sober. Iris smiled reassuringly at him.

"What did you say?" he asked, his voice sounding raspy and his eyes serious.

Iris lifted one shoulder and looked out the window. "I love you."

Trey scooted closer to her on the bench and grabbed both of her hands, forcing her to look at him. "We've known each other less than two weeks. Our relationship started when I stole your ice cream and then bribed you to be my girlfriend."

Iris winced. When he put it that way, it sounded pretty bad. "I know. But I can't help it. I wasn't planning on falling in love with anyone. I didn't want to. I hated love. I hated men. I hated the thought of ever having to put my trust in another human being again. I swore I'd never gamble on my happiness again. Ever.

"But you stole my ice cream. You forced me to be your girlfriend. You drove me everywhere on your motorcycle. You like me best when I dress like a wild woman, even when you prefer the way I'm dressed now. You're the only one who's ever seen the real me."

When Trey didn't say anything, Iris continued, "Look, I'm sorry, but I love you. I don't care if it's crazy. I don't care if it's wild. I don't even care if you have a problem with it. It's just the way it is," she said, her voice rising and her eyes turning bright.

Trey shook his head and then pulled her over to sit on his lap. "I'm so relieved, because I loved you first." He leaned in to kiss her.

Iris gasped and pulled back before their lips could meet. "You did not! I said it first, I felt it first. I own this love."

Trey's eyes glowed with happiness as he shook his head again. "Fine then; when was the exact moment? Because I'll tell you when I fell in love. When you threatened to kill me in that very nice pawnshop yesterday. I knew the minute you pointed that weapon of mass destruction at me that I had finally found the woman who was designed by God especially for me."

Iris sighed in happiness. "You really have a thing for crazy, don't you?" she asked as she kissed him on the cheek.

Trey laughed softly. "It's looking that way. And you? When was your moment?"

Iris snuggled in close to his chest. "To be honest, I think I fell in love with you a little bit each day. I have to admit that first time I saw you standing in front of the ice cream, it was like an electro-shock to the heart. I had felt so dead for months, and then there you were, and my heart started beating again. But yeah, it was the pawnshop. I figured it was serious when I was contemplating maiming. That and the way you kissed me afterwards. I was done for."

Trey hugged her tight for a moment, resting his chin on her head. "I want that knife to go over my fireplace as a reminder of the day we fell in love."

Iris lifted her head for what was sure to be the best, most romantic kiss of her life, only to see three teenage boys looking in the truck window at them. She squawked, pushed Trey's face away, and scooted off his lap.

"Drive, my love. Drive," she ordered, feeling horribly embarrassed but exultant. Trey loved her back.

They grinned at each other as Trey drove into the Thanksgiving Point parking lot. Trey jumped out of the truck and practically ran around to the other side, reaching her just as she hopped out. He glanced around quickly and then pulled her over to the shade of a large tree. "Now, where were we?"

Iris grinned up into Trey's laughing, bright eyes. "Say it first. Say it one more time."

Trey cupped her face in his hands and leaned down close. "I love you," he said and kissed her cheek. "I love you," he whispered. Before their lips could meet, Iris heard her father's voice.

"Iris."

Iris jerked in surprise and looked over Trey's shoulder to see her father and mother standing in front of the entrance to the restaurant, looking appalled.

Iris swallowed and grabbed Trey's hand. She glanced up and knew by Trey's expression that he had caught the looks of horror on her father's face. He didn't look happy.

"Hi, Mom and Dad! Perfect timing. We were just passing the time until you got here," she said, trying to lighten the mood.

Harris Levine looked pained. "Dear, I was under the impression that we were having lunch with *just* you."

Trey looked at her like she was in trouble, crossing his arms across his chest. She frowned up at him and whispered, "Sophie," before walking toward her parents.

"Now, that would just be silly. I would think, since I just introduced you to my new boyfriend last night, that you'd jump at the chance to get to know him. I know I did," she said with a loud laugh.

Trey laughed, but Iris had the impression he was laughing more at her.

Rachel Levine winced but tried to smile. "Well, that's actually what we want to talk to you about. Maybe this is for the best. Why don't we go sit down and we can discuss a few things with the both of you," she said in a careful tone that had Iris raising her eyebrows.

Trey sighed quietly but followed the trio of Levines into the restaurant obediently. Iris was so focused on her parents and Trey that she didn't even notice the décor.

After being seated and ordering, Iris grabbed Trey's hand under the table and decided to take charge. "I think I know what you want to say. Something like, Riley has informed you that I've made some changes and that he's worried and upset. And for some reason that means the two of you need to be worried and upset as well. Am I close?"

Harris looked at his wife first before answering. "Riley did come talk to us after getting back from Utah. He was extremely upset. I've actually never seen him show that much emotion before. He mentioned that you had cut and dyed your hair red, that you were now involved with some construction worker-biker, and that he didn't even recognize you as the same woman he had married. He implied that you had suffered a breakdown of some sort. He was in tears and blamed himself.

He was inconsolable. He begged us to come down so that we could help you. Your mother and I made plans the next day to leave. And to be honest, Iris, we are very worried."

Iris's mouth fell open. She shook her head in shock and turned to look at Trey. His eyes were wide with surprise as well.

"Mom, Dad, you have got to be kidding me," she said, stunned.

Rachel reached across the table and gripped her daughter's hand. "Darling, we waited for three hours in your house for you to come home. We had no idea where you were. When you finally came home, instead of you coming through the door, we meet, um, Trey." Rachel turned to Trey. "Please take no offense, Trey, but you're not the usual type of man that our daughter socializes with. Not that there's anything wrong with bikers or construction workers. But it's just a shock.

"And then when we saw you," Rachel continued, turning to Iris. "You had been riding a motorcycle and you were wearing these crazy jeans and a leather coat. Well, we're just worried. With the annulment and the heartbreak you experienced, maybe this is some dangerous rebound that you're going through to punish Riley for what he did to you."

Iris slowly pulled her hand away from her mother's grasp and looked down at her lap for a moment as she composed herself. Trey rubbed her back softly, but she couldn't look at him. She was mortified.

"First off, before this conversation goes any further, I would like to insist that Trey be treated with the respect and courtesy that would be afforded to the man I'm in love with. You always treated Riley like he was a prince, when in fact, he was a dirt bag. Trey, on the other hand, is respectable, honorable, and a truly good man. Let me assure you that, while Riley is right in that I have made a few changes, mostly cosmetic, he's very wrong in assuming that I've had a mental breakdown. I think I would rather use the term, 'emotional resurrection.'"

Harris sputtered and scooted his chair closer to the table, holding his hand up to interrupt his daughter. Iris shook her head and kept going.

"And to assume that my relationship with Trey is a dangerous rebound is insulting. That I would use Trey in that way is inconceivable."

Iris turned and looked sadly into Trey's eyes. "Trey, you're not a rebound. It's just that I've finally found you."

Trey reached over and pushed a curl behind her ear. "I know, sweetheart."

Iris took a big breath and looked up to meet her parents' eyes. "I came to Alpine to get away from all of the gossip and the pity and the humiliation. You know the smear campaign Riley and his family waged to save his reputation. He's a weak, horrible, cruel man who has used a façade to fool the world. He certainly fooled me. I'm shocked that you would even allow him into your home, let alone believe a word he said after what he did."

Iris took a breath to calm herself. "But I'm your daughter. You can trust me. I want you to know that I'm telling the truth when I say that Trey is unique. He's exceptional, he's funny, and smart, and he loves me. Not for the way I can help his career or make him look good. Just for me."

Harris Levine looked from Iris to Trey and shook his head. "Well, what do you have to say about this?" he said, finally speaking to Trey.

Trey rested his hand on the back of Iris's chair and looked Harris in the eye, then spoke. "Appearances can be deceiving. I understand that. I know that our relationship might seem out of the ordinary. You're looking at me and all you can see is a construction worker who rides a motorcycle. But what you can't see is that I'm honest and hardworking and I love your daughter. I would cherish her, and take care of her, and I can promise you right now that I would never break her heart."

Iris smiled in delight and leaned over to kiss Trey on the cheek. "See?"

Harris and Rachel still didn't look convinced. The waitress brought their food, and Iris looked down in surprise to see that she had ordered steak. She never ordered steak. She must have been seriously stressed out. She looked around at everyone else's entrees and frowned. Her mom and dad had ordered scallops, and Trey had ordered the salmon. Trey saw her eyeing his salmon and raised his eyebrow. "Would you like to trade?"

Iris smiled hopefully and nodded. Trey switched plates, and Iris dug in. She was so glad everything was squared away. She'd have to find a way to introduce her parents to Stan and Sue while they were in town. She pushed the sleeves up on her cashmere sweater as she reached for a roll. Looking up a second later, she saw her parents staring in horror at the tattoos on her arm. Iris blushed and thought about pushing the sleeve back down, but it was too late. She looked at Trey, but he was looking at her parents' horrified faces with a look of defeat on his own. She had just messed everything up.

"Are those tattoos? Riley mentioned tattoos, but we didn't believe it," her mother whispered, covering her mouth with her napkin.

Harris looked furious and turned his anger on Trey. "Did you encourage her to do this?" he demanded.

Trey put his napkin on his plate and shook his head. "No sir, I did not encourage her to get tattoos, but once she had them, I thought they were very nice," he said, sealing his fate.

Iris sighed wearily. "Trey had nothing to do with the tattoos. They're henna, which means they're temporary. They've already faded. You should have seen them last week. They'll be gone in three weeks at the latest. I thought they were fun. They are fun."

Harris's jaw tightened as he looked into his wife's worried face. "I'm sorry, Iris, but I think Riley is right. You're gone for a few weeks and you're doing things you never would have done before. You're dating a man you never would have considered dating before. And I'm worried. You say this isn't a rebound, but to start seeing a man one week and then jump to being in love the next is just ridiculous. That's not love, Iris. That's lust. Love, real love, takes time. It takes effort. This isn't it.

"I want you to come home for a while to get your head on straight. You can leave the truck and everything you've bought here, and you can fly home with your mother and me this afternoon. We can leave right now."

Iris opened her mouth, but her mom jumped in before she could make a sound. "Listen to your father, Iris. He's right. I dated him for a year before I knew I was in love. You dated Riley for one year and were engaged for two. This is crazy. And you're not crazy. You're the most sane, responsible, intelligent young woman we know.

"We have a wonderful counselor we want you to meet with when we get home. She's helped many people deal with emotional trauma. She told us before we left that you could be developing a dual personality because you can't deal with Riley's unfaithfulness. Iris, I think she's right. It's time to come home."

Iris felt a tear slip down her cheek, and her hands started shaking.

She stood up and pushed away from the table. "You're wrong. You are so wrong."

She turned and walked blindly out of the restaurant, hoping Trey was following her. Reaching the truck, she realized he wasn't behind her. She opened the door and pulled herself up into the cab. Lying on the seat, she started to cry in earnest. She didn't know how long she lay there, crying, but what seemed like hours later, Trey finally opened the door to the driver's side and climbed in. Iris sat up and Trey pulled her into his arms. He held her until she stopped shaking.

Before she could embarrass herself further, Iris pulled some tissues from the glove compartment. She blew her nose and then turned the mirror down, to try and wipe some of the mascara off her face.

"What a mess," she said, not talking about her face.

Trey continued to rub her back and nodded. "Let's go for a ride, okay?"

Iris nodded tiredly. She didn't want to go home in case her parents showed up and tried to convince her she needed to be committed. And she was too emotional to go to the job site. She leaned her head tiredly on Trey's shoulder as he drove. Closing her eyes, she tried to forget the last half hour had ever happened. When Trey finally stopped and turned the truck off, she found herself in the mountains.

Trey pushed her hair out of her face and smiled at her sadly. "That was pretty harsh. Your parents make Sophie seem like a sweet little angel."

Iris smiled weakly and rubbed her arms, feeling cold. "I'm so sorry you had to hear all of that. I don't even know what to say."

Trey nodded and looked out the window. "After you walked out, your mom and dad and I had a little conversation. From where they're sitting, all of the facts add up to an emotional breakdown. Where I'm sitting, it just means that you and I finally found where we're supposed to be. With each other. But they're not buying it. They want you to go home. There's some banquet in a few nights that one of their friends is throwing. You oversaw the renovation of part of their house, I guess. Your parents want you there. These people want you to be there too, I take it."

They sat in silence before Trey added, "I think you should go."

Iris gasped and looked at Trey in shock. "I don't want to go. I don't want to leave you."

Trey looked pained and ran his hand through his hair. "I don't want you to go either. But you need to. Go to this party. Spend some time with your parents. Heck, see the counselor too. Just do whatever it takes to reassure your parents that everything is fine. And then come back to me."

Iris groaned and leaned her head on the dashboard. "But what about the restaurant? I've made a commitment to Rick and Sharon. "

Trey sighed. "I've got all your instructions and all of your drawings and sketches. If I have a question, I can just call you. It won't be easy, but I'm willing to do whatever it takes so that your parents are okay with you being here. Being with me."

Iris raised an eyebrow. "Really? Because you could have easily told them during lunch that you own half of a successful construction company and that you're independently wealthy. You let them believe you're a biker. You could have set the record straight," she said accusingly.

Trey blew out a breath and shrugged. "I guess I'm a little prideful. I don't really want your parents to judge me on material possessions. You shouldn't go to the highest bidder. I want them to judge me on my integrity and my love for you. Because that's what should matter."

Iris nodded her head and took her hair down, rubbing her scalp and letting her hair fall around her shoulders. "You're right, Trey. It's kind of funny, but they're the ones who set me up with Riley. He was the older son of one of their best friends. I was never interested in him growing up, because he was five years older than me, but after I graduated and started working his parents and my parents orchestrated the whole set up. They constantly told me how perfect he was for me. It almost felt like an arranged marriage at times.

"This is going to shock you, and you'll probably think less of me, because I know I think less of myself because of it, but I'm not sure that I was ever really in love with Riley. He picked me for whatever his reasons were, but I just naively went along with the plan. Because when I compare what I felt for him to how I feel for you, they're not even the same emotion."

Trey's eyes warmed and he smiled at her as he held his arms open. Iris melted into his chest and held him tightly. "Iris, I haven't asked you, but it's been on my mind. Were you and Riley married in the temple?"

Iris shook her head immediately. "It was just another red flag I ignored. He told me that his parents hadn't paid their tithing, and so since his parents couldn't be at the ceremony, he wanted to wait a year and then do the sealing when his parents could be with us. I was such an idiot, I believed him. I didn't want to embarrass his parents of course, so I never asked them. All along, it was his own sins that were keeping him out of the temple."

Trey ran his hand through her hair as the seconds ticked by. "Just another thing I can thank Riley for."

Iris smiled as she felt Trey's heartbeat. "I don't want to go."

Trey rested his head against hers and sighed. "If there was any other solution, I would jump on it. But if you stay, I have a feeling that your parents will never be okay with you being here with me. You're their only child. I can tell how much they care about you. And I know it would hurt you if you weren't close to them. We'll do things their way for now."

Iris sniffed and rubbed her finger down the vertical pattern of Trey's tan flannel shirt. "And what if I jump through every hoop, see every counselor they throw at me, and they still can't accept you or the real me?"

Trey frowned and kissed the top of her head. "Then you have a choice to make."

Iris nodded. "They'll come around, Trey."

Trey leaned his head back against the seat and closed his eyes. "And if they don't?"

Iris sat up and turned to face him. She waited until he opened his eyes and looked at her. "Then I feel very sorry for them, because they'll miss out on getting to know you and the beautiful children we're going to have someday."

Trey's face transformed into a grin and he laughed. "Please tell me you did not just propose."

Iris grinned and shrugged.

Trey shook his finger in her face. "Uh-uh. You might be one or two steps ahead of me, but I'm putting my foot down, Iris. There are certain protocols that I expect you to abide by. Now behave yourself."

Iris grimaced. "I've spent my entire life behaving myself, and all it got me was an annulment and an appointment with a counselor tomorrow afternoon."

Trey winced and hugged her before he started the truck. "Everything will be okay, Iris. I have total faith that you'll be able to work a miracle and prove to your parents that you're not some wild and crazy biker woman."

Iris groaned. "Start praying. And Trey, just so you know, what my parents said back there about my being in lust with you and not really being in love with you? That's not true. I mean, well, I do think you're hands down the most attractive man I've ever met. Honestly, I really do. And when you kiss me, it's like . . . oh, how do I describe it, it's like Disneyland, surfing, and jumping out of a plane all at once. Okay, maybe there is a little lust, but there's so much love, Trey. I feel it surrounding me just like that vibe you were talking about. I can practically touch it."

Trey turned the truck off, chucked the keys over his shoulder, and took her arms, pulling her to him. "And that's the only reason I'm letting you go. I feel it too. It's the only thing strong enough to withstand everything everybody is throwing at us. I love you, Iris. And I'm completely fine with your uncontrollable lust. Just don't tell your parents," he said kissing her with passion, sadness, and sweetness.

A few minutes later, Iris pulled away and was surprised to find tears on her cheeks. Trey kissed the tears away. "You'll come back to me."

Iris nodded. "I promise."

Trey found the keys after a moment of searching and finally started the truck. Iris stared out the window silently as they drove slowly home. It was time to pack.

Chapter 22

Maggie, Jacie, and Allison checked each other out before entering the Salon. Maggie knew they looked ridiculous, but she was determined to make a statement to Sophie.

"Okay, let's do it."

Jacie and Allison giggled at each other, before replacing their grins with serious, fierce glares. Maggie opened the door and breezed past a woman from her ward whose mouth had fallen open in shock. Maggie winked at her and then motioned for Jacie and Allison to hurry. The three women walked into the heart of the salon. Two stylists paused what they were doing to stare.

Maggie looked around in disappointment. She didn't want all of her adrenaline going to waste. "Where is she, Jacie? You told us she'd be here. No way am I spraying purple streaks in my hair again. I think you damaged my lungs."

Jacie muttered something and then grinned as she heard laughter coming from the back.

"Perfect. She's taking a break. Follow me," Jacie ordered and walked confidently through the salon toward the back room.

Maggie and Allison hurried to catch up. They went through a doorway to a small room where there was a couch, a fridge, and a small table. Sophie and Macie Jo were giggling over a magazine article.

Sophie looked up as the three women came to stand in front of her. She blinked a few times in surprise and then laughed at them.

"Macie Jo, have you ever seen anything so sorry in all your life? Three grown women playing dress up."

Macie Jo smiled at the three women. "I like your boots."

Jacie smiled. "Thanks, Macie Jo. I'll let you know where you can get a pair. Sophie's just in a bad mood because she wasn't invited to play with us. As a matter of fact, she won't be invited to play dress up with us if she doesn't stop acting like a total and complete brat."

Sophie glared at her best friend and then stood up. "So, what's your deal? Why'd you come all the way down here, dressed like Iris wannabes? Make your point and leave."

Maggie stepped forward, making Sophie take a step backwards. "The boots and jeans are just us. The three of us love them, so get used to seeing boot prints all around Alpine. And just so you know, I've had four women stop me and beg me to know where to get some just like them. Looks like Iris is starting a fashion craze. The colored streaks in our hair are just to tick you off, though. I heard from Iris that you threw a little fit at a family dinner and humiliated her in front of Trey and his parents," Maggie said, her blue eyes sending daggers right at Sophie.

Sophie winced and looked down at her feet. "What a little tattletale."

Allison frowned and grabbed Maggie's arm before she could actually kill Sophie.

"Sophie, let's get down to business. You broke the rule. We only had one. We all agreed to it, and you not only broke the rule, but you took it, shredded it, and flushed it down the toilet. You're welcome to defend yourself, but we're here to talk about your punishment."

Sophie's head reared up in outrage. "That rule was to protect Trey. And that's what I'm doing."

Allison put her finger in Sophie's face and shook it. "No. The rule was that as soon as Trey made *his* choice, everyone would support him and his happiness. That was the rule, you broke it, and now you're going to pay the consequences."

Maggie raised her eyebrow at Jacie over Allison's head. Jacie grinned. "This is why she ruled high school. She's made of steel."

Sophie sputtered. "You've got to be kidding me! If you three wackos think you're going to punish me because I can't stand the idea of some lunatic being with Trey, then you're just as crazy as Iris. Forget it. Get out of here. I have work to do," she ordered, pointing to the door.

"We thought it was only fair to have Iris pick your punishment, but she had to leave town for some family business. So the three of us voted and we all agree that we've come up with the best punishment for you," Allison continued as if Sophie hadn't said anything.

Sophie's mouth looked pinched, and her foot started tapping on the floor. "Not that I care, but just out of curiosity, what did you come up with?"

Allison flipped her blue-streaked blonde hair over her shoulder and put her hands on her small waist. "You have to take care of Iris's cock-a-poo while she's gone. Luke's allergic. Her name is Sally, and she needs at least one walk a day since she has a little weight problem. We've written the instructions for you."

Sophie laughed and shook her head. "Not in this lifetime. What else you got?"

Allison smiled sweetly. "You're getting flames, Sophie. But since your hair is already red, we feel that blue flames on the tips would set it off. Macie Jo will perform the procedure, and Jacie will watch to make sure it's all completely permanent. And that includes straightening your curls so the jagged ends show up."

Sophie's face turned white, making her freckles stand out. "Have you lost your mind?"

Allison shook her head, looking grim. "No, that would be you. Last item of punishment. You're going to apologize. You're going to apologize to Iris and to Trey and to his parents. And you're going to make it good. And Sophie, you'd better mean it."

Sophie sat back down at the table and looked shaken. "And what if I refuse? You can't make me do anything."

Maggie tilted her head and looked at the woman who had been her good friend for many years. "Luke tells me that Stan and Sue are still furious with you. Sam isn't happy with the way you've treated his little brother's girlfriend, either. And Trey doesn't even want to see you or talk to you right now. Your three best friends are ready to throw you over a cliff. Has the way you've treated Iris made you happy? Has it helped Trey one bit? I'm kind of curious as to your motivation. Why would a normally kind, good person act so heinously toward another woman?"

Sophie bit her lip and looked down. "I'll admit that I've been a little harsh, but I'm still not accepting this stupid punishment because my intentions were good. I wanted to help Trey."

Allison shook her head sadly. "The pathway to hell is paved with good intentions, and a woman who can't admit when she's wrong is not a woman I want to be friends with."

Maggie nodded and looked pained. "A woman who would turn on someone who has been hurt and is struggling to find her power and her identity is not someone I would want to be friends with."

Jacie paused, since she had been friends with Sophie the longest. She looked at Sophie with tears in her eyes. "I'm ashamed of you, Sophie," she said and turned and walked quickly out of the salon.

Maggie and Allison looked at Sophie's stricken face a moment longer and then turned and followed Jacie.

Macie Jo patted Sophie on the shoulder and then left her by herself. Sophie sat at the table, staring at her hands for a long time.

Chapter 23

ris had been gone three days, and Trey was dying without her. He worked like a madman trying to get his mind off of her, but it didn't help. Every spare second, his mind and heart were taken up with Iris.

He was grateful Iris's notes were so organized and detailed. The restaurant was taking shape. The sculpture she had ordered from Zach Morris had arrived that morning, and overseeing the placement with Rick and Sharon was a great moment. Sharon sobbed on Rick's shoulder, and if Trey wasn't mistaken, Rick's allergy attack was just pure emotion at having something so beautiful in his very own restaurant. It killed Trey that Iris wasn't here to see it. She should have been.

With the painting almost finished and the flooring to be completed within the next two days, the restaurant was on schedule to be open in two weeks. Trey had already seen a newspaper article on the opening. Nobody had bothered to mention Iris, though. The thought made Trey frown. He and Sam were getting the attention for most of Iris's ideas, and it didn't sit well with him. He was having their secretary contact the newspaper with the corrections.

After walking Rick and Sharon to their car, Trey was ready to call it a day. He hadn't talked to Iris for a day and a half, and he wanted to see how she was doing. She had called him immediately after her first counseling session and had sounded fine, great even. Some of her friends from Seattle had heard she was back in town and insisted on taking her out to dinner to celebrate. He hadn't heard from her since. She was probably just busy.

He made the rounds of all the different subs and got a progress report before heading for his motorcycle.

"Hey, boss. Hold up!"

Trey turned around with a frown to see Donny walking toward him.

"What's up, Donny?" he asked politely.

Donny shoved his big beefy hands in his jeans pockets and looked worried. "I haven't seen Iris around lately. I wanted to give her a poem I wrote for her."

Trey glared at Donny and shoved his radio in his pocket. "Who do you think you are, writing *my* girlfriend poems?" he asked, feeling violent all of a sudden.

Donny grinned and rubbed his chin. "Sorry, but she brings out the poet in me. I feel inspired every time I see her. What can I say?"

Trey clenched his hands and took a breath. "Go get inspired some-where else, because she's *mine*. And my girlfriend doesn't need poetry from anyone but me."

Donny looked unconcerned by that small detail. "Well, I hear that might not actually be the case. I heard from a buddy of mine that she left because you two broke up. I figured if that's the case, then I'd like your permission to ask her out. It would take a real strong man to keep a woman like Iris happy."

Trey started to see red and his hands started to clench and unclench. "That's it," he said and launched himself at Donny.

He and Donny pounded each other for the next few minutes before the plumbing crew and half the electricians were able to pull the two men apart.

Trey ended up with a busted lip, a black eye, and with what was almost sure to be a broken rib. Donny's nose was once again broken, and he also had a black eye and was busy throwing up in the gravel from all of the punches he'd taken to his gut. Where Donny was as strong as an ox, Trey was quick and agile.

Trey grinned as his brother Sam drove up. Perfect timing. Sam jumped out of the truck and ran to his side, taking in the damage. He growled and turned on Donny, handing his radio to a sub standing by.

"You beat up my little brother?" he asked sounding even more deadly than Trey. Trey had grown up being the better looking of the two, but Sam was stockier and no one you'd want to meet in a dark alleyway. He walked purposefully toward Donny, who was standing now, and started rolling up his shirtsleeves. He was more than happy to take up where Trey had left off.

Donny held up his hand tiredly. "Don't even think about it. Trey did just fine on his own. He doesn't need big brother stepping in."

Trey spit some blood in the dirt and agreed. "Thanks, Sam, but we're good. Thanks, Donny, I feel a hundred times better. Mention Iris again though, and I'll kill you."

Donny laughed and then pushed his nose back into place with a slight whimper. "You break up with Iris, and you'll have to kill me to stop me. Tell her I have a poem with her name on it just waiting for her."

Trey glared and stomped forward but groaned as his rib ached. Sam put a hand on his arm.

"What is going on here?" he demanded.

Trey waved all the onlookers away and limped toward Sam's truck. He leaned against the door and sighed. "Sweet little Donny decided to write a poem for Iris because someone told him we'd broken up. That and I think he was just messing with me."

Sam shook his head and grinned. "My little brother fighting over a woman on the job site. And with Donny of all people. He could have killed you."

Trey glared at Sam. "I believe the fight was pretty even, thank you very much. Besides, the bigger they are, the harder they fall."

Sam laughed and reached for a cold soda out of his cooler in his truck. "Here, put this on your eye. You're going to look hideous tomorrow," he said, sounding horribly jealous.

Trey grinned. "Sorry you had to miss most of the fun. It would have been great if we could have tag-teamed him."

Both brothers smiled at each other. Sam shook his head, "Man, it's been so long since I've been in a gratifying fight."

Trey laughed. "Wasn't that junior high?"

Sam punched Trey in the shoulder, making him groan.

"It was high school, smart-aleck. Come on, I'm taking my little brother out to dinner, just the two of us."

Trey grinned. "Sounds great, but let's stop by the instacare first. I think I need my ribs wrapped."

Sam sighed but helped his brother up into the cab of his truck. Donny waved jauntily as the two drove out of the parking lot.

Sam took Trey to Costa Vida after they were done at the instacare. He carried the trays of food to the table while Trey got the drinks. They both dug into their smothered burritos without even saying a word.

"Excellent. There's nothing better than Mexican food after a fight. Why is that?" Trey mused.

Sam grinned proudly at his younger brother. "Are you trying to make me feel bad? I almost wish Donny would fall for Sophie so I could have a go. Was it like getting hammered by a front loader? Dang, that man is huge."

Trey winced feeling his ribs twinge with pain. "Oh yeah. Try two well-aimed front loaders. And thanks for sticking up for me. You're a good brother, Sam. Love ya," he said sincerely.

Sam smiled back. "I'll always be here for you, Trey. You know that."

Trey frowned. "So what's the deal with Sophie? I've been meaning to talk to you about what happened the other day at your house, but I'm not even sure what to say."

Sam looked embarrassed but looked Trey in the eyes. "Honestly? I have no idea what has gotten into Sophie lately. She's irritable one minute and then super loving the next. But regardless, I want you to know how sorry I am that you brought your girlfriend to my home and she was treated so poorly. I had it out with Sophie after you guys left, and she locked herself in our bedroom for two hours and cried. But what I really want you to know is that I like Iris, and I think she's perfect for you. I've never met a woman who could keep you on your toes. "

Trey smiled and took another bite. "You didn't think Allison was perfect for me?"

Sam snorted and shook his head. "Allison is great, don't get me wrong. Beautiful, sweet, intelligent, the whole package. But you need something different. You need a woman out of the ordinary that will keep you hopping. Iris is one of a kind."

Trey smiled sadly and nodded. "I miss her like crazy, Sam. She's only been gone a few days, but I swear I feel like I'm dying without her."

Sam laughed. "Ah, that's nothing. That just means you have it bad.

Totally normal. She'll be back before you know it and you can show off your new tattoos."

Trey grinned down at the tattoos that matched Iris's exactly. "She'll love them. You know she sent painters to my house yesterday? And she had a couch delivered this afternoon. She's decorating my house by phone."

Sam smiled across the table. "Thank goodness. When does she get home?"

Trey frowned and rubbed his sore jaw. "I wish I knew."

Sam took another bite as he studied his brother's solemn face. "Is there something you're not telling me, Trey? You said she had some family situation to take care of back in Seattle. Is it more than that?"

Trey looked up, his usually happy blue eyes bleak and worried. "Her parents are worried about her. They came down to see how she was doing and saw how Iris was dressing and who she had fallen in love with. They think I'm a bad influence on her. They think she's on the rebound from her ex, and they insisted she get counseling. Right now, they're trying to convince her that she's not in love with me."

Sam's face was blank for a minute before it hardened. "The heck you say."

Trey held his hand up before his protective older brother could start a full-fledged rant. "I told her to go. I told her to go so she could convince them that everything's fine, with her and with me. She'll come back to me."

Sam's heart hurt at the anguish on his little brother's face. "Of course she will."

Trey smiled halfheartedly, and they finished eating dinner. They talked about the restaurant and three other jobs coming up and then went over the fight from beginning to finish just for the fun of it. But Sam kept shooting him worried looks, and Trey felt more and more uneasy. What would he do if she didn't come back to him? He didn't even want to think about it.

Chapter 24

ris texted Trey again and sighed. She hadn't heard from him in two days. He'd called her right after she'd gotten to Seattle, but that was it. She'd called him to tell him about the counseling session she'd survived and the friends she was going to dinner with, and then, *bam*. Nothing.

She lay on her bed and stared up at the ceiling. Her condo gave her some much-needed independence and space. She refused to stay at her parents' house. They were trying to micro-manage every second of her time and it was getting on her nerves. When she wasn't with her parents, she was being bombarded with invitations by all of her old friends to go to dinner or shopping. And the job offers were pouring in. Her parents had been busy. She knew they were behind it all. She was starting to feel that slow poison seep into her bloodstream again.

So she'd done everything she could to kill it. She'd gone to every single dinner invitation and smiled her heart out. She'd bragged about Trey and told everybody how in love she was. And every job offer she received, she turned down. No one seemed to believe her when she said she was transferring to Utah.

She was a twenty-four-year-old woman. In the end, it really didn't matter if they believed her or not. She was an independent and strong woman who could and would make decisions for herself.

Her parents' constant worry was draining, though. Trey had told her to convince them that everything was fine, and she was trying, but they weren't buying it. She'd seen the counselor twice now. She'd promised her parents to go back one more time, but after that, she was done. It had actually felt great to sit back and tell a complete stranger exactly what happened and how she felt about it. The counselor had nodded her head sympathetically, and that was about it.

Just two more weeks, then she'd be back with Trey in Utah. She had one more social engagement to go to and then she was done: her parents' anniversary party. It meant more time in Washington, but there was no way of getting out of it. It would be held at their beach house on Gig harbor. Everyone would be there. So she'd go, she'd talk, she'd smile, and then she'd leave. She would shut the door on Seattle and start her new life completely free of regrets or guilt.

Turning over onto her stomach, she pulled her laptop toward her. She tapped a button and the new bedroom furniture she was ordering for Trey popped up. The only thing that was bringing her any pleasure was decorating Trey's house for him. This would be her present to him to show him how much she truly loved him. He wouldn't see one invoice. Of course, she was ordering everything according to her taste. Everything except the basement. That would be Trey's man-cave.

She stayed up until one in the morning, ordering everything online and sending emails to the electrician. She wanted him there tomorrow to hang the new light fixtures.

Iris finally shut the laptop and walked tiredly to the bathroom to brush her teeth. Tomorrow was a busy day. She was having a realtor come to list her condo, she had a lunch date with two old college room-mates, and she was going to do her best to finish Maggie's portrait. She'd brought all of the paint supplies and the canvas with her.

Too bad Trey hadn't called. *Again.* If he didn't call her tomorrow or answer one of her texts, she would start worrying. But tonight, she was just too tired.

She went to bed that night, picturing Trey's house in her mind. But in her dream, it was her house, and she and Trey lived there together with their dog, Sally.

Chapter 25

Trey woke up more miserable than he'd ever been in his entire life. Iris had been gone for over a week. He'd finally gotten her on the phone two days before, but she'd been so busy, she could only talk to him for five minutes. And during that five minutes, she'd talked mostly about his house and the furniture. She hadn't mentioned once when she was coming back. And he hadn't asked. He felt sick, but he wasn't going to beg her to come back.

He walked through the house and frowned. It was perfect. Tasteful and refined but casual and fun too. It was just like Iris, and it made him ache for her every time he came home.

Trey stared in the mirror and realized he hadn't shaved for a few days. He was starting to look a little wild, and with his bruised eye now a light brown, he even looked a little scary. Iris would have loved that.

Flopping down on his new living room couch, Trey stared into space. It was Saturday and he didn't know what to do. He didn't want to do anything. If Iris were here, they could have gone down to his parents' house in St. George for the weekend. They could have gone swimming and rock climbing. But she wasn't here. Trey tried to think what he did before he knew Iris, but he couldn't remember. He knew he golfed a lot with Luke and Sam, but other than that, he didn't even care. Life before Iris was starting to fade a little at the edges.

Trey groaned and rubbed his hands over his face. He had it bad. If Iris's parents could see him right now, they would accuse him of having a dual personality. And probably insist he was having a breakdown too. The scary thing was, he'd probably agree with them.

The doorbell chimed and he dragged himself off the couch to see who it was. He was guessing it was either his mom or Sam. Pulling the door open, he blinked at Maggie Petersen.

"You look hideous," Maggie said cheerfully and walked in, turning in circles around his entry.

"I heard Iris was decorating your house, and I had to see it. I love it. Do you mind?" she asked gesturing to his entire house.

Trey shrugged. "Make yourself at home," he said through a yawn. She set down something wrapped in brown paper before walking swiftly toward the kitchen. Trey resumed his position on the couch.

Maggie found her way back to him fifteen minutes later. "I love it! Iris is a genius. It should be in a magazine, it's so gorgeous."

Trey nodded in agreement. "Yep, it really should."

Maggie snorted and walked closer to him. "Buddy, you are a total mess. Do you know that?"

"I do know that, actually. But thanks for pointing it out. I'm going for the Neanderthal look. I hear it's the newest fashion," he said in a bored voice, just wishing she'd leave.

Maggie motioned toward the couch. "Do you mind if I have a seat?"

Trey groaned and sat up on the couch. "Is there something you wanted to talk to me about?"

Maggie nodded, she sat next to him, then scooted to the other side of the couch. He hadn't showered yet.

"I want to talk to you about Iris."

Trey closed his eyes in pain. "I don't know when she's coming back, Maggie. Sorry."

Maggie nodded in sympathy. "Her parents' anniversary party is in nine days. There's no way she can come back until after that. Luke and I were invited, and I was thinking it would be fun if you came with us and surprised her. What do you think?"

Trey stared at Maggie. "Her parents don't like me, Maggie. I don't think that would go over well, me showing up uninvited."

Maggie flicked his argument away as if it were a fly. "She loves you. You love her. You should be there. Look, I think you should come. Rachel and Harris are sending their private plane down for us and

Luke's parents. One more passenger isn't a big deal. It's a quick flight up, and you can be home the next day. And if you play your cards right, she could be on the plane back with you."

Trey felt hope pour through his veins at the thought of going to Washington to bring Iris home. He never should have let her go. For the first time all day, he felt like smiling. "I'll start packing. What should I wear?"

Maggie laughed and clapped her hands. "I knew you'd do it! Wear your nicest suit and, for heaven's sake, shave. Yuck."

Trey laughed and got up to walk Maggie to the door. "Thanks, Maggie. This is just what I needed."

Maggie leaned over and picked up the forgotten package on the floor. "Oh, and here's a housewarming gift. I think it'll go perfectly over the fireplace. "

"Maggie, you really shouldn't have," he said as he ripped the brown paper. In his hands, he held the portrait of Iris that Maggie had painted the year before. She was leaning on a tree, wearing a white filmy dress and looking over her shoulder playfully.

"Iris," Trey whispered, staring as if he were mesmerized.

Maggie sniffed and wiped her eyes. "Your expression right now. You should see it. In case you had any doubts, you are a man in love."

Trey tore his eyes away from Iris and smiled at Maggie. "I could have told you that. Thank you. Thank you, so much. You know, I never even took her picture. I didn't have anything to look at," he said sadly.

Maggie stood on her tiptoes and kissed him on the cheek. "You'll have the real thing soon. Now, go shower, and eat something," she said, letting herself out the front door.

Trey stared at the portrait for a long time before going to look for a hammer and nails. The shower could wait. He had to put Iris where she belonged first.

He grabbed his ladder from the garage and hung the picture over the fireplace. When he was finished, he stood back to make sure it was straight. Perfect. Iris seemed to be looking at him. Trey felt his heart lighten. He would be seeing her soon. In just over a week. He walked upstairs, pulling his shirt off. He'd take the shower and shave.

Iris was getting two surprises. Today, he was going ring shopping.

Chapter 26

Iris twirled in front of the mirror, loving the way the gold and silver dress swished around her hips. She'd never have worn a dress like this before. Although it was modest, it was daring in design. She wished with all her heart that Trey could be here to see her wear it.

She walked over to do her makeup and smiled, knowing that in a few days she'd be with him. She'd been vague on the phone every time the subject of her coming home came up. She wanted to surprise him by driving up to the job site on her own bright red-and-black Ducati. She was having it transported to Utah so it would be waiting in her garage when she got home. She giggled to herself as she applied her makeup. The knee-high biker boots she'd found at a store in downtown Seattle were going to look amazing with her new red leather jacket. As much as she wanted to make her parents happy, she couldn't wait to slip on a pair of jeans and a T-shirt and get back to Utah.

She checked her hair in the mirror, pleased with the waves the stylist had given her, and then went downstairs to join the party. It had started an hour ago, but she wanted to make an entrance. She pasted a wide, happy smile on her face and squared her shoulders. It was time to go to work: reassure her parents, let everyone know she was happy, and then get out of Dodge.

As she glided down the stairs, letting her hand slide down the glossy wood banister, she smiled sadly out the window at the Puget Sound. Trey would love the water. She hoped that her parents would relent and invite her and Trey back to the house so they could really get to know him. She could take him sailing.

"Iris!"

Iris stopped daydreaming and hurried down the stairs to hug one of her aunts. After that, it was nonstop socializing. A half an hour later, she had to go in search of a drink. Her throat was parched from all the talking and she was starting to sound hoarse. That and her cheeks needed a break from smiling. She took a plate of food from one of the servers and a flute of sparkling apple juice in her other and turned to find a corner.

"You look beautiful tonight."

Surprised, Iris looked up to see Riley Shelton standing in front of her, looking elegant and suave.

Iris took a sip of her drink and nodded. "I'm a little surprised to see you here, Riley. Don't you have a date or three?"

Riley ignored the jab and tilted his head to study her. "You look really good, Iris. You look happy, confident, and a little wild. I like it. I think our little break has been good for you."

Iris shook her head. "Go away, Riley," she said, trying to walk around him.

"Not so fast. You don't have a bodyguard around to keep me back now. You're going to listen to me." He took the plate of food out of her hand, giving it back to the server, and then pulled her out onto the dance floor.

Iris still had her drink in one hand and was trying valiantly not to spill, as Riley wrapped both of his arms around her waist.

"Right back where you belong. With me," Riley murmured in her ear.

Iris pushed him away, but his arms were locked and he wasn't moving. "Let me go, Riley. Now," she ordered.

Riley shook his head and gave her what he thought was a sexy look. "Never. Now stop making a scene and just listen to me. We've both changed a lot in the last few months. I think we should give our relationship another try. Your parents tell me that your counseling has done wonders for you. You're practically back to normal. Once you get back into the swing of things again, I think we should have our own party to announce our reengagement."

Iris's mouth fell open, and she shook her head. "I'd rather die than be with you ever again. Now remove your hands and let me go."

Riley stopped swaying to the music and looked down at her with a frown. "It's time to grow up, Iris. Stop acting like a child and let the past go. Just forgive my mistakes and we can move on. Your refusing to forgive me says more about you than my weakness with women says about me."

Iris laughed bitterly and pushed against his chest again. "Yeah, it's all my fault, Riley. Keep telling yourself that. How many women are you stringing along right now? Three? Five?"

Riley rolled his eyes and refused to answer. "If you'll agree to marry me again, I'll get rid of all of them. You have my word on it. But you'll have to do your part. Like I said before, our relationship is a two-way street. You never loved me the way I needed you to. You do your part, and I'll do mine," he promised.

Iris snorted and considered stomping his foot with her heel. "You just love that two-way street analogy. You'll probably have it on your gravestone when you die. But here's the truth for you. Our relationship was never a two-way street. It was a bridge. And your side crumbled, over and over again, bringing everything down. Blaming me and rationalizing your actions is only hurting you. I refuse to take the blame for your infidelities. It's time for *you* to grow up."

Riley looked away from her, sneering, but then his expression changed. He blinked a few times and then grinned almost evilly. "Fine Iris, have it your way. But I insist on a good-bye kiss." Before she could protest, he bent down and leaned her back, kissing her against her will. Iris tried to squirm away, but his hold on her was too tight. Then she remembered the drink she still had in her right hand and she tipped the glass, pouring beverage over the back of his head. She fell hard on the wooden floor of the ballroom as Riley finally released her.

Riley glared down at her as the apple juice ran down onto his face. "You're just not worth the effort," he said. Wiping the sticky liquid off his face, he flicked it at her and stormed away.

Iris groaned as she clumsily got to her knees. Her hip ached where it had smashed into the floor. Two arms wrapped around her waist and pulled her up from behind. She turned to thank whoever it was and saw it was Luke Petersen with Maggie standing next to him.

Iris screamed and threw her arms around both of their necks at the same time. "Oh, it's so good to see you. And Luke, what timing. I wish you had been here five minutes earlier. Riley wouldn't let me go, and then he kissed me, so I poured my drink on his head," she said, laughing and hoping that her parents didn't make a big deal out of it later.

Luke and Maggie frowned and glanced at each other. "Let's get off the dance floor so we can catch up," Maggie said, guiding Iris toward an empty corner in the back of the room.

Iris sighed happily. Her parents hadn't told her Luke and Maggie were coming. She pushed her hair out of her face and grinned at Maggie. "How's Trey? Oh, I miss him so much I can barely stand it."

Luke cleared his throat and looked uncomfortable. "He's been better."

Iris frowned and looked to Maggie. Maggie winced and looked ill. "Iris, we brought Trey with us. Trey saw you dancing with Riley. He saw you two kissing." Iris craned her neck, searching the crowd for Trey. "He left. He's upset, Iris. From where we were standing, it didn't look good. He didn't stay to see you dump your drink on Riley. He thinks you were, um, willingly participating."

Iris gasped and covered her mouth. She scanned the crowd again, looking for a glimpse of Trey anywhere.

"Don't bother. He ran out. He's long gone now," Luke said quietly.

Iris's breathing was shallow and quick. "So he thinks that I wanted to dance with Riley? He thinks that I was letting him kiss me? He thinks I don't love him anymore?" she asked in anguish.

Luke and Maggie nodded solemnly. "That about sums up the situation," Luke said bluntly.

Maggie grabbed her hand. "We saw you dump the drink on his head, Iris. I believe you if you say you didn't want Riley to kiss you."

Iris laughed almost hysterically. "Of course I didn't! I can't stand that man. I begged him to let me go, but I didn't want to make a scene and ruin my parents' party. But when he kissed me I had to do something. He's furious. He wanted us to get back together, but of course I told him that would never happen. And now Trey thinks that's exactly what I was doing," she whispered, shaking her head.

Luke sighed and rubbed his hand through his hair. "This is a disaster. Trey's probably hijacking the ferry right now."

Maggie shook her head and scanned the room. "Is there anyway you can leave right now, Iris? Maybe we can head him off?"

Iris rubbed her cold arms and shook her head. "I've been assigned the first toast in about a half an hour. There's no way I can leave. My parents would throw a fit. But I promise you I'll be in Utah tomorrow afternoon at the latest."

Luke and Maggie looked at her questioningly. "Really?" Maggie asked. "You're really coming back to Utah? Because some of us weren't sure. We were kind of wondering if maybe you had decided to stay in Seattle and go back to your old life."

Iris looked at Maggie like she was insane. "Why would I want this, when I could have Trey?" she asked, gesturing to the crowds of people and the exquisite ballroom.

Luke looked worried still. "Just one problem. Trey. How are you going to convince him that he didn't see what he thinks he saw?"

Iris frowned and bit her lip. "He'll believe me. He trusts me. If I could just leave now," she said glaring at all of her parents' party guests.

Maggie frowned at the people too. "Just grab a microphone and make your toast. I'm worried, Iris. Trey looked devastated. I'm scared of what he might do."

Iris groaned and ran for the small stage where the band was playing. She waved her arms to make the band stop and ripped the microphone out of the holder. "Ladies and Gentlemen, may I have your attention?"

The crowd immediately quieted and looked askance. Déjà vu. Most of these people had been at her wedding. Iris laughed weakly as the memory washed over her. Realizing she didn't have a drink in her hand anymore, she motioned for a server.

"Everyone, I think it's about time to start making toasts to my parents, Harris and Rachel Levine. I would be honored to be the first."

Iris waited as everyone who didn't have a drink took one from the servers walking quietly through the crowds. She raised her arm and finally spotted her parents looking pleased as they walked toward the stage.

"Mom, Dad, if you'll join me on the stage please."

Harris and Rachel walked smoothly up the stairs to join their only child, putting their arms around her waist and kissing her on the cheek.

"To twenty-eight years of marriage. To faithfulness, kindness, integrity, and love. I have always dreamed of having a marriage as sweet and good as my parents have. I know I will, because I won't settle for anything else. I love you Mom and Dad. To Harris and Rachel," she said and lifted her glass high before taking a sip.

Her Mom and Dad kissed and hugged her, and then the microphone was snagged by one of her dad's golfing buddies. She blew kisses at her parents, smiled for the crowd, and then disappeared into the throng of people to find Maggie and Luke.

They were standing in the same place, at the back of the room, talking to a tall, well-dressed man. She walked to Maggie's side and grabbed her arm.

"Sorry to interrupt, but let's get going. We've got a man to catch," she said, pulling Maggie away from the man.

Maggie cleared her throat as she dug in her heels. "Iris, Trey's here. He didn't leave."

Iris let go of Maggie's arm and slowly turned to stare into the solemn, sad eyes of the man she loved.

He looked magnificent. His custom-made, navy blue suit formed perfectly to his shoulders and hips, and the conservative red tie had him fitting in with every other guest there. His usually tousled light brown hair was combed back, making him look like a politician.

"I thought you'd left," she whispered walking to his side and reaching out to touch his arm.

Luke and Maggie disappeared into the crowd, leaving them alone.

Trey glanced over her head at the crowd laughing at some joke about her parents. "Is there somewhere we can go that's a little less noisy?" he asked.

Iris nodded and motioned him to follow her. She walked out of the ballroom and down a well-lit hallway until she reached a door. She opened it and walked outside, waiting until Trey followed her.

Pointing toward a pathway that led past the pool and down toward the shoreline, she said, "Why don't we walk down by the water?"

Trey nodded and followed her in the moonlight. Iris's heart ached, knowing what Trey must be thinking and feeling. He looked so quiet and reserved. He looked different.

When they reached the water, she stopped walking and looked up at the moon. Trey stood beside her, not touching, but close.

"I didn't want Riley to kiss me, Trey. He dragged me onto the dance floor, and since I didn't want to ruin my parents' party, I didn't throw a fit. But when he kissed me, I dumped my drink on his head, and he dropped me to the floor. You can ask Maggie and Luke."

Trey nodded his head and sighed. "Luke texted me what happened. I believe you," he said simply.

Iris sighed in relief and grabbed Trey's hand. "Oh, Trey, I was just sick. When Maggie and Luke told me that you saw Riley kissing me and that you had taken off, I didn't know what to do. I wasn't even supposed to do the toast for another half an hour, but I grabbed the microphone and just started talking. I don't even really know what I said. I just knew I had to find you and explain everything."

Trey nodded his head slowly and stared out over the water. "What exactly does your dad do that he can afford a home in Seattle and a beach home with a ballroom on a little island?"

Iris blinked and frowned at the quick change in subject. "Um, its a little company called Microsoft. He's been there almost since the beginning and has a lot of stock in the company."

Trey nodded again. "We've actually been here for about an hour. I've been watching you. Dancing, talking, and smiling at everyone. You're comfortable here . . . in this life."

Iris frowned as Trey let go of her hand to put his hands in his pockets. "Well, I was raised this way. And all the people at the party are people I've known forever. But just because I was raised with all of this doesn't mean that I won't be happy in Utah. It doesn't mean I won't be happy with you," she said, inching closer to him.

Trey smiled sadly. "Doesn't it? All I know is that when you left you practically disappeared. I hardly heard from you. And when you did call, we hardly spoke before you had to go. From where I'm standing, it looks like your parents were right. You came to Utah to have a little fling, but now that you're home, well, you're home," he said sadly.

Iris shook her head and grabbed his arm. "No, Trey! No, that's not it at all. I was just doing what you told me to do. I was assuring my parents that I'm not completely insane, and then I had lunch or dinner with everybody I knew, to make my parents happy, yes, but also to say good-bye. I'm moving back to Utah, Trey. I'm already packed!"

Trey stared into her bright-green eyes, looking as if he wanted to believe her, but couldn't bring himself to. He glanced over her hair and dress and looked almost pained.

"You don't look like the girl I met at the grocery store. I think your parents are right, Iris. I think you're out of my league."

Iris's face crumpled as she realized Trey was trying to say good-bye. "Don't do this, Trey. Don't just give up on me. Please," she said, not wanting to beg.

Trey turned away from her and walked closer to the water. When he turned back, he looked furious. "Do you think I want to, Iris? Do you think I want to let you go? This is killing me. I love you. I love you more than I've ever loved any other woman, and I know every woman I meet from now until the day I die will come up short because they're not you. I love you, but I love you enough to know that this is where you belong. Not with me."

Iris groaned in pain and hugged her arms, feeling cold and hollow. "The only place in the world I truly belong is with you."

Trey breathed in deeply and let it out slowly as he walked back toward her. He took her in his arms, hugging her tightly, and then leaned down to kiss her forehead.

"Be happy, Iris," he said and then walked back to the house, leaving her alone with the night.

Chapter 27

ris walked back to the house an hour later, bypassing the ballroom. She walked up the back stairs to the room she used when she stayed at the beach house. All of the guests were being ferried back to the mainland at ten, but she and her parents would spend the night. She wondered if Maggie and Luke were still downstairs mingling. She wondered where Trey was.

She stripped off her dress and hung it up and then went into the opulent bathroom. Everything was glass and white marble. She turned the water on in the bathtub and waited until it was full. Lowering her cold body into the warm water, she wished the water could somehow warm the coldness that had taken root inside her chest.

As her body slowly thawed, she stared at the water and went over every word Trey had said. She went over everything she had said in response and wondered if she could have said anything different that would have convinced him. The only thing she regretted was that she hadn't told him she loved him.

Iris stayed in the water until she was cold again. Stepping out of the tub, she wrapped herself in a large, warm bath towel. As she dried off she glared at the mirror. She wasn't going to let him walk out of her life.

She got dressed in her pajamas, grabbed her phone, and then sat on the bed. If Trey thought it would be easy to dump her, then he was kidding himself. She happened to be a strong, wild woman, and there was no way she was giving up on him even if he had given up on her.

She texted him one short line. "I'm coming for you, so watch out."

Setting her phone on the side table, Iris glanced at the suitcase she had packed for the weekend at the beach house and wished Trey could have seen all of the packed boxes back at her condo. It didn't matter. She had a big day tomorrow and needed to get some sleep. She was moving home.

Chapter 28

Iris walked into breakfast at eight the next morning and smiled brightly at her parents. They were just finishing the paper as she sat down. She scooped up some steaming scrambled eggs and grabbed a slice of toast.

"What a party," she said as she took a bite.

Harris lowered the paper and glanced expectantly at his wife. She lowered her section of the paper and looked back before turning to her daughter.

"It was a great party. Best anniversary party I think we've ever had. Wouldn't you agree, Harris?"

Harris nodded and smiled genuinely at his wife before turning to look worriedly at his daughter. "We didn't see you toward the end, though. Weren't you feeling well?"

Iris shrugged and took a sip of orange juice before answering. "I needed to get to bed early. I'm moving back to Utah today," she said quietly but firmly.

Harris Levine's face hardened as he crossed his arms over his chest and leaned back in his chair. "I thought we were done with all of that nonsense, Iris. You've been home for a few weeks, and you're just now getting back into the swing of things. You haven't even gone back to work yet, which has me worried. And although your counselor tells us that you're doing well, considering the emotional trauma you've been through, I think a trip to Utah would be detrimental to say the least."

Iris took another sip of juice and smiled complacently. "I only came home because I wanted to assure you that I was fine. And I've done that. I've put my life on hold because I love you and I know that the annulment was hard on you too. But I'm done putting my life on hold. My life is not here anymore. My life is in Utah with the man I love."

Rachel made a clicking noise with her mouth and stood up. Harris looked up at her and nodded firmly. "Yes, Rachel, get the envelope. We need to put an end to this once and for all."

As her mother left the breakfast nook, Iris finished her toast, looking out the window at the Sound. She would miss seeing the boats in the morning, but the mountains would make up for it. Harris studied his daughter's calm face with concern, his fingers tapping on the table.

Rachel walked back in the room, holding a large manila envelope in her hands. "Now, before I tell you what's in this envelope, I want you to know that your father only did this out of love and concern for you. You're our only child and, yes, I admit that we might be a little overprotective. But after you see the pictures, I think you'll agree that we were justified."

Iris silently held her hand out for the envelope. Her mother gave it to her and sat down, looking sad and tense.

Iris opened the envelope and pulled out a stack of eight-by-ten glossy photographs. She smiled as she saw Trey sitting at a table at what looked like Applebee's. He looked thin and unhappy. She moved the front picture to the back of the pile and looked at the next one. He was standing to greet somebody. By his expression, he was surprised. She moved the picture to the back and held up the next picture. A woman with red hair. It wasn't a good shot though, because the picture was out of focus. She moved it to the back. Yep, a red-haired woman with straight hair, cut into jagged spikes on the end and dyed a bright blue. Iris's eyes widened as she quickly moved the picture to the back. In this picture the photographer had obviously moved to get a better shot of the woman's face. Iris's mouth fell open as she realized it was Sophie Kellen.

Sophie. With blue flame-tipped hair, cut almost exactly as her hair had been cut. By Trey's face, he was stunned speechless. Sophie's expression was contrite and serious.

Iris covered her mouth with her hand as she noticed what Sophie was wearing. A rock band T-shirt and faded jeans, tucked into a pair of the sorriest looking excuse for boots she'd ever seen. Obviously Maggie hadn't told her where to shop. She quickly pushed the picture to the back of the pile and smiled as she saw Trey hugging Sophie. The next picture was of Trey kissing Sophie on the cheek. Iris studied Trey's beautiful face and sighed wistfully. If all went according to plan, she'd be seeing him very soon. There was only one picture left. She pulled it closer to her face as her mouth dropped open. Trey was showing Sophie a ring box with a large diamond ring in it. Trey's face looked excited and happy and now Sophie's face was shocked.

Iris gently put the pictures back in the envelope and turned toward the large windows facing the water. Trey had bought a ring. Trey had bought *her* a ring. Iris felt all the coldness that had wrapped around her heart disappear. Trey loved her. He had acted like a complete idiot the night before, but she would forgive him. He had come to Washington to ask her to marry him.

Iris laughed and covered her mouth with her hands as she walked toward the glass and leaned her forehead against the cool glass. She was going to marry Trey Kellen. She grinned and felt joy flit through her stomach like a thousand butterflies. She had to get to Trey.

She turned around to leave and realized her parents were still watching her with worried expressions. They were probably thinking she was having a breakdown. She smiled at her mom and dad and sat back down at the table, steepling her hands together in a businesslike matter.

"Thanks for the pictures; they made my day. What your private investigator took pictures of was Trey having lunch with his sister-in-law, Sophie Kellen. She's married to Sam, his older brother." A giggle slipped between her lips as she wondered what Maggie and Allison did to get Sophie to cut and dye her hair.

Harris and Rachel looked disgruntled and furious. Harris was firm. "There was a question of whether or not this woman was a relation of Trey's. Our investigator was very thorough, though. The woman Trey is kissing and hugging is obviously some trashy biker woman he probably picked up in a bar."

Iris laughed and shook her head. "There was a bet to see who could set Trey up with the perfect woman. Maggie chose me, and Sophie, the woman in the picture, picked a different woman. Trey and I got together and Sophie had a hard time accepting Trey's choice. You see, she took one look at my boots and jeans and was convinced that I wasn't good enough for her brother-in-law."

Rachel looked confused and upset. "But she's dressed horribly! She looks worse than you did that night we came to your house."

Iris sighed, happily. "Actually, I look pretty good in my jeans and boots. Sophie looks kind of silly. But I'm just being mean. Sophie broke a rule. She couldn't or wouldn't accept that Trey had chosen me. So she threw a fit. She invited me to her home to meet Trey's brother and his parents and then threw Riley in my face and my hair and tattoos. She embarrassed me in front of Trey's parents and made me cry. She crossed the line. So Maggie, you know, Luke's wife? She and a couple of her friends came up with a punishment for Sophie for being so mean to me. Looks like she had to get her hair done just like mine."

Iris picked up the envelope and grinned. She was keeping these pictures. Someday, when she was blue she would get these out and laugh herself silly.

Harris held up his hand. "Wait, this woman, the one Trey is hugging, the one who looks like a truck stop waitress, thinks *you're* not good enough for Trey? Does she know who you are?"

Iris stood up with the envelope under her arm. "She might actually have a point, Dad, but I'm not letting that get in my way. I love Trey, and I'm going to marry him. I'll call you when I get to town," she said and headed for the door.

Harris and Rachel stood up and moved to block the door. "No, Iris. We insist that you stay here, where you belong," Rachel said, her voice pleading. "This is your home, and as your parents we know what's best for you. So things didn't work out with Riley. Your father knows a wonderful young man at work that he's impressed with. He's intelligent, educated, comes from a good family, and lives here in Seattle. We'd like you to stay for a few more months and give it a try. I won't stand by and see you throw your life away."

Iris stared at her parents blocking the door and took a deep breath. She was strong. She was independent. And yes, she was even a little wild. She could face down her parents.

"Those are valid concerns. And if I were sixteen, you'd be right to insist. But I'm twenty-four and I've done things your way my whole life. I'm an adult, a very sane adult by the way, and I have the right to make my own decisions. If you can't accept that or support me, then I know a very good counselor who can help you deal with disappointment.

"But regardless of how you feel, I am leaving today. I am moving to Utah. And one way or another, I'm going to live the rest of my life with Trey Kellen. If you choose to not be a part of my life because of some misplaced pride in who is good enough for whom, then that's your loss. My decision is about love. That's what matters."

Iris stared her parents down, not blinking until they slowly moved out of her way. Neither one said a word as she walked to the front door, where her bags were waiting for her. She took one last look at the house she loved. She hoped she would see it again someday. Maybe with her own children.

Iris opened the door and walked out. She had one more stop before she left for Utah.

Chapter 29

Trey stared gloomily from inside the restaurant at the crowd congregating in the parking lot. Rick and Sharon were standing with three of their children, getting ready to cut the ribbon. Waiters passed out appetizers to the crowd of reporters, friends, and everybody who had helped build the restaurant. There were even a few curious people who were just interested in a good restaurant. Donny was standing on the edge of the crowd with a few of the plumbers. Probably hoping for a glimpse of Iris.

Trey glared at Donny and scanned the crowd again. Sophie and Sam had arrived and were talking to Sharon. Sophie still had her hair done in blue-tipped flames. She was told she couldn't change it until Iris saw it in person. Sophie didn't know it yet, but she might look ridiculous for the rest of her life. He smiled at the thought and looked for any other familiar faces. He spotted his mom and dad and, standing beside them, Luke and Maggie.

His smile faded. He knew they were there to check up on him. They'd gotten back from Seattle yesterday afternoon. Luke's parents had wanted to eat lunch on the wharf before leaving, but Trey hadn't been in the mood. He'd sat in his hotel room alone, more depressed than he'd ever been. The flight home had been a silent torture.

He couldn't stay here, not with all the reminders of Iris. That's why, after the ribbon cutting and the quote for the newspaper, he was heading out of town for a long time. He'd already told Sam not to expect him at work for at least two months. He had plenty in the bank, and he was ready to spend it. If it took every penny he had to forget Iris, he would. Surfing in Australia might be a good place to start. After that, he didn't care. As long as it wasn't Alpine, Utah.

He leaned tiredly against the cool window, knowing he should go join Sam and Rick and Sharon, but he couldn't get his feet to move. He blinked as he heard the sound of a high-powered motor. Recognizing the sound of a Ducati, he straightened. As far as he knew, he was the only man in Alpine who owned a Ducati. Scanning the parking lot in front of the restaurant, Trey spotted the bike. It was smaller than his with custom red flames on the sides. Flashy, he thought with a sneer.

The driver stopped the bike and climbed off awkwardly, as if he weren't sure what he was doing. Trey snorted and crossed his arms, ready to laugh at the poor idiot if his bike fell over on the pavement. The man figured out the stand and then stood up.

Trey paused and watched, unblinking, as he realized that the driver was a woman. Definitely not a man. She was wearing black leather pants, black knee-high boots with silver buckles going up the sides, and a bright red, fitted leather jacket. The helmet was beautiful. Glossy black with phoenix wings in red.

Trey swallowed. Then he saw Donny. He was practically running toward the motorcycle and the rider. The woman slowly lifted the helmet off her head and held it in her arms as the glossiest, silkiest Cherry Coke hair tipped in bright-red flames fell around her shoulders.

Trey's heart started beating again. She had come back to him.

Iris scanned the crowd. She was looking for him. Her mouth turned up in a grin as she spotted someone. She waved at Donny as she passed him, eating up the pavement in her boots as she made her way toward the front of the crowd.

Trey's eyebrows shot up as he watched Iris tap Sophie on the shoulder. He hoped that the opening of Rick and Sharon's restaurant wasn't ruined by a biker chick brawl. He opened the door and walked outside, coming to a stop behind Iris and Sophie, in case he needed to jump in.

"I like the hair, Sophie, but the boots are just sad."

Sophie whipped her head around, her blue-tipped hair flying, and glared up at Iris, who was at least four inches taller than she was. Sophie opened her mouth, about to say something snide, and then clamped her lips shut. She took a deep breath, looked at her husband who was grinning at her, and then looked Iris in the eyes.

"Iris, I want to apologize to you. I judged you wrongly, and I was very unkind to you. I'm very, truly sorry that I embarrassed you at my home and treated you so poorly in front of Trey's parents. I hope that you'll forgive me." Her chin was high, but she sounded sincere.

Trey was proud of his sister-in-law.

"I will accept your apology on two conditions," Iris said. "One, I want to know why. From everything I've heard about you, you're supposedly the nicest person in Alpine. Maggie told me that you know what it's like to feel like you don't fit in. So why?"

Sophie closed her eyes as if she were in pain and looked at her feet. "I was scared for Trey. When he loves, he gives everything. He doesn't hold back. I couldn't stand to see him get hurt again. Then you show up, all wild and crazy. I took one look at you and saw heartbreak. I'm sorry, Iris. I misjudged you."

A circle of people had formed around the two women, and Trey felt a little embarrassed that his emotions were being picked apart in front of them.

Iris put her hands on her hips and looked over Sophie's head. "Well, people are surprising. I didn't dump Trey, but he sure dumped me good and hard the other night."

Sophie's head whipped up and her mouth fell open. "No! No, he wouldn't. He bought a . . ." she clapped a hand over her mouth as she realized what she was about to say.

Iris cocked her head and continued. "Yep, he sure did. Left my heart dying in the sand and walked away without even looking back."

Trey noticed Donny standing to the side of the circle of people, his eyes now glowed with what could only be hope. Trey groaned.

"So, um, what was your second condition?" Sophie asked curiously.

Iris lifted up a hand to study her scarlet red fingernails. "I want you to keep your hair like this for at least a month."

Sophie stamped her little foot on the ground and bunched her hands into fists. "No! Do you know how embarrassing it is to be a stylist and have everyone stare at you like you're a freak?"

Iris laughed and shook her head. "So stop looking so embarrassed about it. Have some fun, Sophie. Wear your hair with pride and stop looking like you lost a bet."

Sophie rolled her eyes and flipped her blue tipped hair over her shoulder. "By the way, your cock-a-poo misses you, so you can come pick her up anytime today. She'll be waiting for you."

Iris nodded her head regally and then turned to walk away. Donny had other plans, though.

"Iris, my dream, my angel. Now that you're a free woman, I would love to have the chance to take you out to dinner. I promise you I know how to treat a woman."

Trey growled and pushed his way to Iris's side. "She's not going anywhere with you. I told you she's my girlfriend, and that's the end of it. Now back off."

Trey turned to Iris, ready to embrace her, but she was staring at him as if he were a complete stranger. She walked around him and took Donny's arm. "Donny, let's go over here where we can talk privately," she said, ignoring Trey as if he were a speck of dirt.

Iris put her elegant hand on Donny's arm, and Donny gave Trey a triumphant smile, which caused all the blood to rush to Trey's face.

"Iris, knock it off. Leave Donny alone and let's talk."

Iris turned slowly and stared at Trey as if he were insane. "Excuse me? Did you just tell me to knock it off?" she asked icily.

Trey swallowed nervously as he realized how angry she was. Donny didn't seem to like being interrupted, either.

"Trey, you had your chance. You messed up and now it's my turn. Back off or I'll break two more ribs," he said glaring at Trey menacingly.

Iris looked up at Donny in horror.

Trey held up his hands for peace. "I'm sorry, Iris. I set you free in Seattle because I thought it was the right thing. I thought maybe you had decided you didn't want to come back to me after all."

Iris looked anguished for a moment before she schooled her expression. "Well, if you had once replied to any of the hundreds of texts I sent you, you would have known, wouldn't you?"

Trey stared at her, his mouth open.

Iris smiled at his expression. "Well, get used to seeing me around town, because I'm here for good. And just know that you dumped the one woman who would have loved you forever, with all her heart. I would have given you everything I had to give. You threw me away. You got cold feet, and you gave up on me." The last sentence came out as a sob. Iris covered her mouth as Donny led her away.

Trey stared in shock as the woman he adored walked away from him, her red-tipped hair swinging in the wind, looking like it had caught fire.

"You are the biggest idiot I've ever known," Sam said, throwing his arm around Trey's shoulders. "Still heading to Australia to surf?"

Trey shook his head and started smiling. "Heck no. She came back to me. I just have to figure out how to get her back now," he said.

Sam let out a whoop and pumped his fist into the air. "That's the spirit, Trey. Only one problem. Donny will kill you if you get near her."

Trey shrugged, still grinning as he stared at Iris showing Donny her new motorcycle. "I can take him. It's Iris I'm worried about. I bet you she's mine again in three days," he said as happiness filled his heart.

Sam laughed and pounded Trey on the back. "I'll take that bet. I say it's a week minimum. Now let's start the show. Rick and Sharon are about to pass out they're so excited. Plus, I'm hungry."

Trey did his duty, clapping when he was supposed to clap and smiling when he was supposed to smile, but as soon as it was over, he was gone. He had a list of things he needed to do before he matched wits with his girl. And first thing on his list was to get his phone back from the store. He'd taken it in because the screen had cracked. He'd been using his work phone to call Iris. She had been texting the wrong phone.

Trey picked up his phone and stopped by the grocery store to get some Chunky Monkey. It seemed only right to eat their favorite ice cream while he read everything he had missed. Sitting down at the kitchen counter, he immediately forgot about the ice cream.

She had texted him two hundred and thirty-six times. Trey rubbed his hand over his hair and knew he was in trouble. An hour later, his heart was light. One more text left to read.

I'm coming for you.

Trey frowned. Knowing Iris, that might be a threat. But when she had faced him down today at the restaurant, she hadn't looked violent. She'd looked hurt. Besides, he still had the knife. He'd mounted it on the fireplace right under her portrait. He looked up at the woman he loved one more time before heading for the garage. Sophie wasn't the only one who would be apologizing today. It was his turn.

Chapter 30

ris grinned at Sally and noticed that she had gained at least another pound. Sophie and Sam had probably spoiled her rotten while she was gone, even though Sam swore that they had both faithfully walked her.

"It's time for doggy diet food, Sally. You leave me no choice. I've missed you, so you get all the treats you want today, but tomorrow you're turning over a new leaf." Sally stood on her short hind legs and laid her paws on Iris's skirt.

The sound of a motorcycle turning down her street had Iris hiding a smile. She knew Trey would show up sooner or later. She schooled her face and tried to look as bored and uncaring as possible. Trey hopped off his bike and sauntered up the front walk, smiling at her as if he were a king. Iris rolled her eyes and threw a treat for Sally to catch. Iris had to look away. Sometimes looking at Trey was like looking at the sun. She noticed Maggie watching them from her porch. "Now, what happened to the black leather pants and your red jacket?" he asked, standing on the top step and leaning nonchalantly on the post.

Focus, Iris reminded herself. She couldn't blow this before she got an apology. Iris looked back at Trey and rolled her eyes. "I have many sides, Trey. Leather is just one. I've discovered I like cotton too. Besides, leather gets hot after a while." She threw a treat for Sally to catch. Trey studied her and smiled approvingly. "Well, I like the new look. Very feminine. Very sweet."

Iris smiled politely. "How kind of you to say so."

Trey looked like he was waiting for her to say more. When she didn't, he came and sat next to her. "Iris, I read the texts you sent. I'm sorry I didn't read them earlier. My phone was broken."

Iris huffed and leaned back in her chair. *Sure it was.*

"No, seriously," Trey said, reading the disbelief on her face. He leaned in, trying to get her to look him in the eyes. "When I called you in Seattle, it was from my work phone. I never would have ignored you."

The sincerity in his voice made Iris look at him. Trey smiled as their eyes met. *You're losing it,* Iris thought, but she couldn't look away.

Trey broke the silence first. "I especially liked your last text." The teasing in his voice brought Iris back to her senses.

If he thinks he can waltz in and I'll melt into his arms, he's got another thing coming. She couldn't let him get to her. Iris crossed her arms. "I'm glad you liked it. But after I sent it I realized you stole my knife. I'm having Donny buy me a bigger one as we speak." Trey's smile faded as he tried to figure out if she was serious. "Iris, come on. I love you. You love me. You came back, so let's just take it from here. I'm sorry that I hurt you. Please, please forgive me."

There was no teasing in his voice now. He almost sounded pained. Iris glanced at him and noticed again how gorgeous he was. It was so hard being firm. "You didn't have faith in me, Trey. How can I have a relationship with a man who dumped me because he didn't trust me or my love for him?"

Trey stood and walked to the edge of the porch, shoving his hands in his pockets. "I've been burned before. I guess I have a hard time trusting. I know you love me. But is it enough to give up your glamorous life and settle down in Utah?" Trey ran his hand through his hair, distressed. Iris closed her eyes, willing herself not to give into emotion. If she started crying now, she'd just have to shoot Trey and be done with it.

"I'm a strong, independent woman, Trey. I need a man who's strong, wild, and crazy enough to believe me when I tell him I love him."

Trey turned back toward Iris and nudged her foot with his. "I do."

Iris sniffed and hid her misty eyes by turning her attention to Sally.

Trey edged a little closer. "So, why did you come back if you don't love me anymore?" Iris could hear the teasing in his voice, but she rose to the bait. "Oh, I love you. I love you so much it hurts to breathe most of the time. Just looking at you right now makes the protons and the neutrons in my body want to jump out of their cells. But I'm mature enough to realize that a relationship needs more trust, faith, and a little backbone."

Trey crouched in front of Iris and placed his hands on her arms. "Our relationship is all of that and more." Iris kept her face straight, looking bored. A muscle twitched in Trey's jaw. He stood up and paced the porch, looking more and more frustrated. "What do I need to do to prove that I trust you, love you, and have faith in you?"

Iris shrugged. "I don't know, Trey, but if I were you I'd start figuring that out."

Trey growled and turned around to look at the mountains. "Fine, but if I see you anywhere near Donny, I'm going to kill him and then I'm coming after you."

Iris laughed and shook her head. "You know there's no other man for me. It can only be you, Trey."

Trey whipped around and stared at her as if she were insane. "Why are you playing games with me, Iris?"

Iris looked offended. "Put yourself in my shoes. You've been cheated on and hurt. You've survived an annulment and all the humiliation that comes with it. You do something wild and crazy and fall in love again. You pledge your love to this person and almost immediately you get dumped. How should I feel?"

Trey looked at his boots and sighed. "I guess when you put it like that, I sound like a complete jerk. You deserve better, Iris. You really do," he said and turned to leave.

Iris's mouth fell open in surprise. *He's giving up too easily.*

Trey was halfway down the porch steps when he turned around. Iris shut her mouth quickly, trying to look bored again. "Oh, before I forget, I need all the invoices for all the furniture and lighting and painting that you did on my house. I like to pay off my debts."

Iris shrugged. "You'll be cold in your grave before you see one receipt. Consider it a gift from a woman who adored you."

Trey smiled wickedly. "Correction. *Still* adores. Adios, Iris." He whistled as he walked to his bike and hopped on, driving away as if he hadn't a care in the world.

Iris stood up, glaring after him as he drove down the street and disappeared around the corner. Maggie hurried over. "Well? How'd it go? Did he beg for forgiveness? Is everything okay?"

Iris shook her head. "Sometimes, I just hate men. He sort of apologized. He sort of begged for forgiveness. But when I said he'd have to prove it, he just sauntered off like he had to go golfing or something. I swear I'm going to kill that man."

Maggie laughed and relaxed. "Nah, he's just playing you. His brain is probably going a million miles an hour trying to come up with something big enough to win you back."

Iris smiled and laughed lightly. "He better be, if he knows what's good for him. Hey, come in the house for a second. I have a surprise for you."

Maggie followed Iris to the family room in the back of the house. Noticing a large rectangular shape wrapped in brown paper, Maggie squeaked with excitement. "You finished!"

Before Iris could confirm that she had, Maggie was ripping paper until she held a large, beautifully framed portrait of herself and her son.

Maggie stared silently, shaking her head now and then. She gently leaned the long frame against the wall and stepped back to get a better view, her face glowing with wonder and amazement.

Iris smiled as she watched Maggie take in the portrait, giving her the time and silence she needed.

"I take it you're a Gustav Klimt fan?" Maggie finally asked, her eyes still racing around the portrait.

Iris laughed and collapsed on the couch, knowing Maggie was going to take a while to process. "You could say that. I've always been a follower of Caravaggio and the old masters, but I've been in a Klimt kind of mind frame lately. If it's not your style, I can always do something more traditional."

Maggie finally tore her gaze away from her portrait and looked at Iris in horror. "Don't you dare! This is a masterpiece. I had no idea what to expect from you. Of course I would love anything you did, but this is beyond anything I could have imagined. I'm speechless. Iris, you're just as good as me," she said in a stunned voice.

Iris looked at her in delight. "Stop it, Maggie. Just say thank you, and we'll call it good."

Maggie walked over and took Iris by the arms, literally shaking her. "Listen, you little idiot. I don't know what you've been doing these last few years decorating houses and restaurants and mansions and whatever else it is you do, but you should have been painting. You're a master."

Iris gently pulled back from Maggie and frowned at her. "I'd rather paint than do just about anything else. I wanted to be an artist, but my parents insisted that I have a stable career. They didn't think being an artist qualified as a respectable occupation. But I do love painting."

Maggie's face shone bright with excitement. "You can paint here, in Alpine. Spend the next year painting, and I'll show your work to my agent. We'll have a showing at the gallery. Iris, you're going to be huge."

Iris looked back at the portrait she had done of Maggie and Talon and shrugged. She loved how it turned out. She had felt so constricted in Washington, and all of her feelings had come out in paint. It wasn't half bad, but could she be an artist full time? The idea was way too crazy. Way too wild. It was perfect.

Iris smiled. "Sure. This is a new chapter of my life. I might as well try, right?"

Maggie laughed and grabbed Iris's arms, swinging her around in a circle.

"Hey, I knocked, but . . ." Luke walked into the room, holding Talon in his arms. He stopped as he caught sight of the portrait of his wife and child. Iris watched silently as adoration shone on his face. Maggie walked to his side and touched his arm.

Luke shook his head and cleared his throat but found he couldn't talk. He turned away until he had his emotions under control and then turned back around and grabbed his wife in his free arm, kissing her hair and holding her tight.

"I want that painting, Iris. I will pay you whatever you want for it. I will give you anything you ask. But that painting is mine," Luke said.

"You're my favorite cousin, Luke. Of course it's yours. No charge."

Luke covered his mouth with his hand and looked at Maggie, stunned. Maggie nodded and wrapped her arms around her husband's waist. "Have I mentioned how much I love your cousin, Luke? I love her enough to forgive her for being a better artist than me."

Luke grinned and kissed his wife. "Maybe not better. How about different? Iris is a lot like her painting: kind of wild, kind of beautiful, and completely unique."

Iris sighed happily as she picked up the painting and put it in Maggie's hands. "Enjoy."

Luke and Maggie walked out of the house, already arguing about where to hang the portrait.

Iris followed them out onto the front porch. She sighed happily. It felt good to be home. Now, if Trey would just hurry up and prove his devotion. Too bad he was the one who insisted on protocols being respected. He'd never forgive her for being a pushover. It was so hard to not fling herself into his arms, but it would be better in the end. Iris walked back into the house with her dog and shut the door. Tomorrow was a new day. She couldn't wait to see what Trey would come up with.

Chapter 31

Trey drove his motorcycle for a couple hours, trying to figure out what to do. He had to do something extraordinary to win Iris back. He pictured her, five years from now, raising little plumber babies who looked just like Donny.

Trey frowned and pulled into a gas station. As he filled his bike and tried not to breathe in the fumes, he thought. *What is the most important thing to Iris?* Besides him of course. The answer came as he twisted the gas cap back on. Her parents. Trey grimaced as he thought about Harris and Rachel Levine. Making friends and connecting with people had always been easy for him. And now, the two people that he really needed to impress hated him.

Bringing Iris's parents around would be the perfect way to prove his devotion to her. But the Levines would never listen to him. Trey grinned as he thought of two people they might listen to. Starting his bike, he turned it toward his parents' house. It was time to get serious.

Chapter 32

It had been two days since Iris had challenged Trey to prove his love for her and she hadn't seen any sign of him or his proof. She was bored, so she decided to walk down to the salon to pick on Sophie. Sauntering into the salon, Iris was greeted by a perky blonde.

"You have to be Iris."

Iris smiled and nodded, wondering what Sophie had been saying about her.

The blonde woman ran around the front desk and threw her arms around Iris's neck, making her stumble and gasp in surprise. "I'm Jacie," the woman said as she let Iris go and stepped back.

Iris recognized the name and laughed. "Okay, gotcha. Jacie of the Famous Four. The one who came up with the bet."

Jacie blushed. "Guilty. I have been wanting to meet you forever, but then you went out of town."

Iris sighed. "Yeah, I had a family situation to take care of, but I'm back for good now."

Jacie motioned behind her. "That's what Trey said. He's just finishing up, but you can go back if you want to."

Trey is here? What in the world is he doing? Iris's eyes widened, but she nodded her head. She followed Jacie to the far corner of the salon and saw Trey in a seat with Sophie standing behind him.

"This is so juvenile, Trey. It's like you're an eighth-grader," Sophie said, shaking her head in consternation as she rubbed his head with a towel.

Trey's face brightened as he spotted Iris in the mirror. It was just a flash of recognition; he then composed himself and talked to Sophie as if Iris wasn't there. "You sound like a grandma, Sophie. Don't you remember what it was like to be young and in love? To feel like you would do anything, be anything just to be with that one person in the world who made you feel more than alive?"

Trey was putting on a show. Iris felt her heart melt, but she couldn't weaken. "Sophie, I need my nails done. Oh, Trey, I didn't see you there. Here for a little trim?" she asked in an uninterested voice

Sophie looked back over her shoulder and sighed tiredly. "Great, the whole circus is here. You're just in time for the big reveal, Iris."

Trey smiled in the mirror at Iris as Sophie whipped the towel off his head to reveal bright white tips covering Trey's hair.

Iris's mouth fell open. Stayed open. Wouldn't shut.

Trey laughed at her expression and stood up, running his hands through his wet hair and making it stand up in spikes. He stepped closer to her. "Iris, I'm trying to figure out how to prove to you how much I love you. I got my hair done as a symbol showing that I will be wild and crazy when it comes to loving you."

Iris gulped and concentrated on holding her ground. He looked like a rock star. A gorgeous, insane rock star. She could imagine what her parents would say. She cleared her throat and gave him her most alluring smile. "Wow, Trey, it looks amazing. If your hair is a symbol of all that, then you should keep it like this for the rest of your life."

Iris had to hold in a giggle as she watched Trey frown and lean down to look in the mirror. He winced but turned to face her with a smile firmly in place. "For you, anything, Iris. Do you really need your nails done right now? If they can wait, I'll show you what I've been working on for the last two days."

Iris looked down at her perfect nails and shrugged. "They can wait."

Trey leaned down to kiss Sophie on the check and then took Iris by the arm. Iris waved at Sophie and Jacie over her shoulder as Trey led her to the back parking lot. Iris looked around expecting to see his motorcycle.

"Where's your Ducati?"

"Oh, I traded that in yesterday," Trey said, guiding her toward a minivan.

"We're going to need a family car, Iris."

Iris felt her face go slack in horror. "You traded in the Ducati? For *this?*"

He opened the passenger door of the generic, white minivan. "As soon as you accept that my faith and trust in you is absolute, we're going to be very busy starting a family. Hop in, my lady." Iris felt numb as she climbed into the van.

"The Ducati is gone?" Trey nodded sadly and buckled her seatbelt for her since her arms didn't seem to work anymore.

"I didn't know how else to prove my love, Iris. There's only one thing that comes close to my love for you, sweetheart. I had to prove I'd sacrifice anything to be with you."

Iris swallowed, feeling awful. "Your Ducati?"

Trey nodded solemnly. "Yep. That's how much you mean to me. Man, I miss that bike."

Trey shut the door and walked around to the driver's side. They drove in silence to Trey's house.

Trey's front yard was taken up with landscapers who were busy laying sod. Iris covered her mouth with her hand as she realized that the sod was being laid around a flower bed of bright-red flowers spelling her name out. Trey had landscaped his yard with her name right smack in the middle. He was insane.

Iris got out of the minivan on shaky legs. Trey put his arm around her shoulders and pulled her in close. "Isn't it beautiful? What better way to prove to the woman I love that she's the only one for me than by saying it with my yard."

Iris nodded her head silently and wished she had a couple aspirin, but she kept her voice bright. "Trey it's really nice. Thank you for, um, doing this. And for the hair too. I've never been so . . . touched." Trey grinned and nodded.

"I knew you'd love it, but that's not really what I wanted you to see. Come inside," he said, pulling her up the front walkway.

Iris took a deep breath, wondering what horrors awaited her. Trey pushed open the front door and ushered her inside. Iris's eyes adjusted to the light, and she looked around, not knowing what she was supposed to be looking at.

Trey pointed at the ceiling of the two-story, vaulted entry. Iris tilted her neck to look and yelped. Someone had painted angels on Trey's ceiling. And they all had her face. Iris shook her head, feeling the tackiness ooze down the walls and cover her in slime. Trey was killing her.

"So what do you think? I had to pay this guy double to get it done so fast, but where there's a will, there's a way. Iris, I want you to know, that I will stop at nothing to prove to you my undying devotion. And I have to admit, it's kind of fun too. I never realized how creative I was until you forced me to look inside myself. This is the most fun I think I've ever had."

She struggled to hold in a laugh as she said, "Wow, Trey, this is a lot of love." She had to bite her lip to keep a straight face and wondered how upset he would be when she had the ceiling repainted.

Trey narrowed his eyes at her. "So I've done it? Is this all I have to do? Am I forgiven?" He tried to look relieved as he asked the question, but Iris could see disappointment tugging at his eyes. He hadn't revealed his grand finale. She could play along a little longer. "Well, of course I forgive you, Trey. But it's the proof I need. The hair, the Ducati, the sod, and these amazing, flame-tipped Iris Angels you have going on up there are a good start, but I have to admit, I was hoping for something bigger. Something transcendent. Something extraordinary."

Trey looked at her with a half-smile. "You know what, Iris, I had a feeling you were going to say that. You are a strong, independent, wild woman and nothing this ordinary could impress you. That's why I have one more trick up my sleeve."

Iris looked down at her feet until she could compose herself. "I knew you had it in you, Trey. A man who is willing to steal a poor, heartbroken woman's ice cream is a man who will do anything to get what he wants. I just hope that you want me as bad as you wanted that Chunky Monkey."

Trey's eyes sparkled at her, and he looked like he was about to burst out laughing, but he held it in. They stood there grinning at each other for a minute before he shook his head.

"The way I feel about you, Iris, goes so far beyond my feelings for Chunky Monkey that sometimes I forget to breathe. All other women are Late Night Snack compared to you. I'd do anything to get you back. *Anything.*"

Iris laughed but enjoyed the compliment more than it deserved. "I don't think I've seen your *anything* yet. But I'm looking forward to it."

Trey stared at her with approval and reached out slowly to take her hand in his. He kissed her knuckles softly, sending a warm shiver down her back.

"Iris, you are one tough woman. Be here tonight at six o'clock for the grand finale. And if you wanted to wear that cute green skirt you had on the other day, I wouldn't mind at all."

Iris smiled and leaned toward Trey, as if to kiss him. "I will be here. Would you like me to bring anything?"

They were inches apart. Electricity sparked between them. "Just you, my dear. Just you," Trey said. He sounded distracted as his eyes jumped from her eyes to her lips. Iris leaned in closer and then pulled away. Trey looked disappointed.

Iris yawned and covered her mouth with her hand. "All of this excitement has worn me out. I better let you get back to your preparations," she said as she walked to the front door

Trey sighed but pasted a smile on his face. "Better take a nap, sweetheart. You're going to need it."

Trey dropped her off at her house and then took off. He said he had a list of things to do for the big dinner.

Iris flopped on her couch and laughed to herself. Trey was a stinker. He was taking her challenge and being naughty. But she loved him for it. It was so him. She had four hours until dinner. *Time to start painting.*

Chapter 33

Iris thought about her almost kiss with Trey the rest of the afternoon. She was anxious to get his grand finale over with so that she could close that space. It seemed like years since she'd kissed Trey. Unable to wait any longer, Iris left her house and drove to Trey's, arriving five minutes early. The electricity she had felt between her and Trey earlier surged through her body.

She checked her reflection in the rearview mirror and straightened her clothes before climbing out of the truck. Trey might have been ridiculous before, but Iris felt that whatever came next was all seriousness.

She walked to the front door and rang the doorbell. The seconds passed slowly and Iris felt her legs tremble as she wondered what would be on the other side of the door when it finally opened.

Iris knocked again before the door opened. Rather than Trey standing on the other side, Iris was shocked to see her parents. Iris gasped and threw her arms around her parents' necks. "What are you doing here? What are you doing in *Trey's house*?" Harris smiled warmly and pulled her inside.

"All in good time. Come in, Iris, Trey's ready to serve dinner."

Rachel and Harris escorted their daughter into the dining room and seated her. Iris scanned the dining room she had designed in taupe, cream, and burgundy. Everything looked the same. She glanced at the ceiling, hoping Trey hadn't gone crazy with cherubs in here. Nope, clean as a whistle. She prayed her parents hadn't bothered looking up when they had arrived.

She frowned as her parents sat across from her. They were both smiling and looked happy. Something was seriously wrong.

"Mom, Dad . . ."

"Iris! I'm so glad you're here!" Sue said. She walked briskly into the dining room, carrying a large covered pan in her hands. She set it expertly on the table and leaned down to kiss Iris on her cheek.

"Sweetie, you look amazing. So glad you're home. We missed you." Sue sat down next to Rachel.

Iris was too shocked to speak, but she was spared from answering as Stan entered the room carrying two baskets of rolls in his hands. He set them down and came over to kiss Iris's cheek as well. He turned to Iris's parents. "Harris, Rachel, I don't know how you did it, but you raised the most extraordinary woman. It's no wonder Trey is so in love with her."

Harris and Rachel looked pleased by the compliment. "Stan, coming from you, that's high praise. Knowing Trey as we do *now*, it seems to Rachel and me that we've never seen two people more suited to each other. We couldn't be more pleased that these two have finally found each other."

Iris's mouth formed an O as she stared at first her parents and then Trey's parents and then her parents again.

Trey walked in, took one look at Iris face, and smiled contentedly. "Now the party can start."

He set down a steaming bowl of couscous and walked over to Iris, kissing her respectfully on the cheek.

"I hope you don't mind, but I invited our parents. I thought it would be a good idea for our families to get to know one another."

Iris nodded, and realized her mouth was still open. After forcing her mouth shut, she cleared her throat.

"I think that's a brilliant idea, Trey. So far, it looks like they're getting along fine."

Trey laughed and shook his head at her as Sue, Stan, Harris, and Rachel jumped in, trying to top each other with how much they enjoyed each other's company.

Trey sat down beside Iris and took her napkin, laying it in her lap for her.

"Our parents have already made plans to go on a cruise together this spring. Isn't that right, Mom?" Trey asked.

Sue looked ecstatic. "We can't wait. Harris and Stan want to go Mediterranean, but Rachel and I are thinking South America. What do you think, Iris?"

Iris blew out a breath and shook her head, still confused and in shock.

Sue smiled knowingly at her. "You're too nice to pick sides. That's just like her, isn't it, Rachel?"

Rachel quickly agreed and came up with three other good qualities that she insisted Iris had.

Iris turned and stared wide eyed at Trey. He was already studying her with laughing eyes. Iris immediately relaxed. This was it. This was his big gesture. Trey had won over her parents. She pushed back from the table and walked to stand behind Trey's chair. She leaned down and wrapped her arms around Trey's shoulders, kissing him passionately on the cheek, and whispered in his ear.

"You win. You did it. You slayed the dragon."

Trey turned his head and grinned at her. "Are you sure? Because I can keep going if you want me to."

Iris shook her head quickly and laughed. "No, no! This is perfect." When she sat down in her seat again, she smiled brightly at both sets of parents.

The meal went smoothly. As soon as it was all over, Stan, Sue, Harris, and Rachel decided to leave at the same time. Harris and Rachel took an extra minute to hug and kiss their daughter, looking at her with more approval than she'd seen in a long time.

As soon as the door shut, she turned on Trey. "What did you do?"

Trey held his hands up and walked backwards toward the family room. "I will admit nothing. You just need to accept the fact that I happen to be a very charming and likeable kind of guy."

Iris laughed and shook her head. "And your parents? Best friends with my mom and dad now? Traveling together? Something funny is going on." Trey sighed happily and pulled Iris down onto the couch in front of the fireplace. Iris finally looked up and gasped. "That's me! That's the painting Maggie did last year," she said, jumping up to get a closer look.

She turned back and looked sweetly at Trey. "You hung it over the fireplace. *With my knife.*"

Trey grinned and waited until she joined him on the couch again. "So I'm truly forgiven?"

Iris rested her head on Trey's shoulder and nodded her head. "Who could resist those Iris cherubs? I don't know who would be strong enough to withstand their power."

Trey laughed and wrapped his arm around Iris's shoulder. "If you only knew how many art students from BYU are desperate for money, you'd cry."

Iris grinned and looked up at him. "Someday, you will tell me how you drugged my parents, shipped their bodies to Utah, and then forced them to be nice."

Trey shook his head. "I doubt it."

Iris punched him on the shoulder but sat up quickly as she heard violin music coming from the kitchen. She whipped her head around and stared at three strange men in tuxedos walking through the dining room toward them.

"Trey!" She stared at the men, who were playing a romantic Latin piece she'd heard before.

She reached out to tug on Trey's shirt, but he was gone. She turned. Trey was kneeling in front of her holding a black ring box in his hand. He stared at her, his eyes completely serious now as she took in the importance of the occasion.

"Iris, my love, I would be the happiest man alive if you'd do me the great honor of being my wife."

Iris took in a shaky breath and let it out slowly as she reached for the box. She slowly opened the box revealing the same ring her father's private investigator had taken pictures of. She smiled at the ring and then looked into Trey's eyes.

"As if you could stop me," she said and threw her arms around Trey's neck, knocking him over and sending the ring rolling under the couch.

Trey laughed, fished for the ring, pushed it onto her finger and then shooed the violin players away with his hand.

And then, when they were finally alone, when there were no more surprises and no more interruptions, Iris finally got the most romantic kiss of her life.

Chapter 34

Sophie sipped her Fresca as she stared hard at the doors of Costa Vida. She calmed her breathing and looked at her watch for the eighth time in five minutes. They were late. Or they weren't coming. Sophie bit her lip as her foot started tapping uncontrollably

The last six months had been hard. Good in some ways, but painful in others. And all because of a stupid bet between her and Maggie. Okay, maybe not because of the bet. Because of her. Sophie winced as she thought back on everything she had done and said to Trey and Iris. Her pale cheeks blushed in embarrassment. It's normal to act like a brat when you're nine. Acting like a brat when you're in your late twenties? Not socially acceptable unless you're a housewife on a reality TV show. Being a bratty housewife in Alpine didn't fly too well.

Sophie stared sadly at all of the groups of friends surrounding her and sighed heavily. She'd had all that. She'd had the most perfect group of friends a woman could ever ask for. Jacie, her best friend throughout her life, had been distant and busy ever since she'd declared war on Iris. Sophie had assumed that just because they were best friends that meant that Jacie would automatically side with her. Instead, she'd been ashamed of her.

Sophie closed her eyes at the painful memory and took another sip, drowning her sorrows in grapefruit-flavored soda. And then there was Maggie. She looked up to Maggie more than anyone. Maggie was fearless, loving, kind, and so good. Maggie was everything she wanted to be, and Maggie had chosen her to be one of her friends. Sophie had been honored. She was still in awe of the woman who had overcome so much. She'd been so flattered when this talented, amazing woman had insisted that they be friends. And she'd messed it all up. She'd been so sure that she knew what was best for Trey. She'd let her pride destroy their friendship.

Sophie squirmed in mortification as she thought of the way she'd acted. She pushed her red hair out of her eyes and glanced at the doors again, willing them to open—willing her friends to walk through the door and join her for dinner like they had so many times before. She glanced at her watch and saw that everyone was now ten minutes late. No one had ever been late before. They'd always jumped at the chance to spend time together. Allison had always been the first one there, smiling and munching on nachos.

Sophie swallowed a sudden wave of grief as she thought of her friendship with Allison. Their relationship had definitely had its ups and downs. She'd hated Allison in high school, but now, Allison was one of her most favorite people. Allison was the one she called when she wanted a kind word. Allison was the one she called when she needed help. And Allison was the one who had stood in front of her that day in the salon and had passed down her punishment.

Sophie cringed as she remembered the blue tips Macie Jo had put in her hair. She'd taken her punishment, though. She'd done everything she was told she had to do. Trash her hair, apologize, wear those stupid ugly boots. Everything. She'd eaten so much humble pie she was about to burst. But things weren't back to normal. Their monthly get-togethers had fizzled out. Their easy friendship was anything but easy now. And she was exhausted. She didn't want to live another day without her friends. And all because of Iris.

Sophie's mouth tightened automatically. Iris *Kellen* now. Sophie stared off into space as she recalled Iris's wedding to Trey. They'd been sealed in the Timpanogos Temple, and the whole town of Alpine had been invited to their reception. And her bridesmaids had been Maggie, Jacie, and Allison, of course. Sophie had stood on the sidelines and smiled as if everything was fine and wonderful. But it hurt.

Iris acted as if they were friends now, but Sophie knew that Iris was still baffled by what she'd done and was on her guard around her. Sophie sniffed and looked down at her folded arms. She didn't blame her. She'd let her love for Trey and her protective instincts take over, and she hadn't cared who she'd hurt or the damage she'd inflicted. In hindsight, she now knew that Iris was actually really pretty cool. She was smart, funny, beautiful, and kind. She was everything Trey deserved. And by the way Trey floated around Alpine, grinning his head off, she knew Iris was the woman meant for her brother-in-law. Iris made everyone around her happy.

Sophie wadded up a napkin in her fist. She'd been so stupid and hard headed. But they wouldn't even let her make it up to them. She'd invited everyone here tonight for dinner, her treat, and no one had even bothered to come. Sophie blinked back hot tears and stood up, reaching down for her purse. She was moving. Forget Alpine. Forget everything. She would just take her husband and little boy and move to Arkansas. No one there would know what a brat she had been. She'd make a new start and make new friends.

Sophie whisked a tear away and walked toward the door, hoping she could keep her tears back until she could reach her car.

The door suddenly whipped open, and Maggie, Jacie, Allison, and Iris stumbled through the doors, laughing and grinning.

"Hey Sophie! Sorry we're late. Iris called and needed a ride, and then Allison insisted she needed a ride too," Maggie said looking over her shoulder at the two women.

Sophie's heart beat fast and she sniffed back a few more tears and pasted a smile on. "Oh, that's no problem. I've got us a table over here." She motioned and turned around quickly to wipe her eyes and headed back to the table she'd just abandoned.

Jacie hurried and grabbed a seat next to Sophie. "Tonight was the perfect night for a Girls' Night Out," she said with a grin and a shake of her head, sending her bright silver earrings dancing.

Maggie, Allison, and Iris took the other seats around the table. Sophie looked up and sent a timid smile to her sister-in-law. Iris smiled happily back at her. Sophie took a deep breath and let it out slowly.

"So what's going on with everybody? I haven't seen you guys in ages," Sophie said, smiling tremulously.

Jacie raised her hand. "Uh, maybe we should get our food first?"

Maggie shook her head. "No, I can't wait. Let's tell Sophie," she said, hopping up and down in her seat.

Allison cleared her throat shyly and looked down at her lap before smiling at Sophie. "Sophie, I want you to be one of the first people I tell. I'm having a baby." She said the words quietly, with such a look of joy and awe on her face that Sophie's tears she had forced back came back with a vengeance.

Sophie squeaked and jumped up, running around the table to throw her arms around her friend's shoulders. "Allison, congratulations! You and Will are going to have the most beautiful baby in the world. Oh my goodness, when are you due?" She demanded, kissing Allison on the cheek before finding her seat again.

Allison laughed, her cheeks rosy and her eyes bright with happiness. "This summer. I haven't told Will yet though. I want a creative way to do it. I don't want to just blurt it out as soon as he gets home. You guys are the experts here. I need some advice," she said, her eyes going soft at the mention of her husband.

Sophie's eyes lit up and she sat up excitedly. This she could do. As she began to speak, though, she was interrupted by Iris.

"Hold up there. I've got some news of my own," Iris said, glancing nervously around the table.

All eyes locked on Iris. Sophie noticed Maggie looked so pleased she was about to pop. She must already know something. Sophie stared at Iris and noticed that Allison wasn't the only one glowing

"I'm pregnant too." She laughed softly, looking surprised and scared at the same time.

Allison and Jacie were the ones to jump up this time, running around the table to hug and kiss Iris until she was completely red in the face.

"I'm so glad we can be pregnant together!" Allison said as she sat down. "We can complain about fat ankles and acne together."

Iris laughed and ran her hand through her dark hair. "I am scared to death. I'm going to need everyone's help to survive this," she said, letting her eyes rest on everyone at the table and ending on Sophie.

"Especially you, Sophie," she said quietly.

Sophie blinked in surprise and glanced around at the women who were smiling at her.

"Me?"

Iris nodded and turned her chair to face her fully. "You're such a good mother. Everything comes to you so naturally. Trey thinks you're practically perfect. And motherhood is the one thing I don't want to mess up. Will you help me?"

Sophie looked down at her hands in her lap as a couple tears fell down her cheeks. She nodded her head, but couldn't speak. Two arms wrapped around her tightly, and she started crying harder. Then she felt even more arms wrap around her as all of her friends surrounded her.

A few minutes and a lot of tissue later, she stared at Iris. "Are you crazy, Iris?"

Iris grinned and nodded promptly. "Yes."

Sophie snorted and shook her head. "Then yes. I will help you. I'll be right there with you through everything. I promise," she said seriously.

Iris smiled gently at her and grabbed her hand lying on top of the table. "Good. Now let's get some food. I'm eating for two."

All of the women got in line, talking, giggling, and handing out advice. Maggie stayed at the rear, next to Sophie.

"I love you, Sophie."

Sophie turned her head and stared at Maggie and walked into her open arms. Maggie hugged her hard for a few moments before pulling back. "But no more bets. Deal?"

Sophie let every last ounce of pain and regret roll off her shoulders as she grinned at her friend. "Deal."

"Now about that years' worth of free salon services you owe me. Do you guys offer waxing? Laser treatments? Botox?" Maggie asked with a sparkle in her eye.

Sophie glared at Maggie and shook her head. "Hmmm. I'll see what I can come up with. I've got time tomorrow morning."

Maggie laughed and hugged Sophie again. "No hair revenge, Sophie. How about a trim instead?"

"Whatever you want, Maggie. But I might like shoving needles in your forehead." Sophie relaxed and smiled happily as she moved up in line. Life was good again.

Epilogue

Sophie sniffed as she studied the Iris cherubs on Trey's ceiling and wondered why Sam had never been romantic enough to paint cherubs of her somewhere in their house. Sam was going to have to step up his game.

She walked to the back of the house and out the patio door to the backyard. She watched all of their friends and family surround Trey and Iris as they celebrated their first wedding anniversary. She scanned the crowd and made a beeline for the guest of honor.

Sophie walked right up to Donny and snatched the baby out of his arms. "Stop hogging the baby, Donny." She turned to the baby and cooed, "Come here, you little chunky monkey. You know you love your aunt Sophie best."

Donny glared at her but decided not to make an issue out of it. "Iris told me just a minute ago that Katana loves me best."

Sophie snorted and shook her head. "Donny, she says that to everybody. Tell him, Macie Jo."

Macie Jo wrapped her arms around her husband's middle and laughed. "It's true, sweetie. Come on, they've got barbecue ribs. I promise you'll get to hold her again before we have to leave."

Donny and Macie Jo headed for the tables laden with mounds of food, leaving Sophie alone with her niece.

"Now, Katana, look at that. Have you ever seen two people more in love?" she asked, pointing her niece's face toward Trey and Iris standing together with their arms wrapped around each other's waists. Behind

181

them was a brand-new Ducati painted a bright red. An anniversary present from Iris to Trey.

"Now remember, true love conquers all. Even evil witches," Sophie said with a delighted giggle and walked toward her husband. Every now and then, she loved being wrong.

Book Club Questions

1. Should Iris have given Riley another chance? Why or why not?

2. In Trey's past, he's always fallen for women who were emotionally unavailable. Is this just another way of playing it safe?

3. Is the saying true, "Once a cheater, always a cheater"?

4. Were Iris's parents out of line? Or were they just being protective?

5. Why did Trey really get cold feet?

6. Were Maggie, Jacie, and Allison right to punish Sophie? And was the punishment fair?

About the Author

Shannon Guymon is a big believer in happy endings. Scarlett really should have been happy with Rhett, and it's a darn shame Leo and Kate didn't float safely into New York on the Titanic. Alas, since she can only control her own imagination, happy endings are found in *Never Letting Go of Hope, A Trusting Heart, Justifiable Means, Forever Friends, Soul Searching, Makeover, Taking Chances*, and *The Broken Road*. Find out more at shannonguymon.blogspot.com.